SPLIT SECOND

I heard the crack again. Sherry glasses slid slowly and soundlessly off the young man's tray, somersaulting to the floor. Munchies flew up into the air. Louise Sugarman blew up. She blew toward me, becoming huge, crashing into me.

At the impact, I turned sideways, slightly away from her. Painlessly sailing through the air, I could see everybody at the other side of the room. The side I had not been watching before. As I floated gently down, I saw the exit door.

The sleek young man stood there with a small black box in his hand. As I sank, oh, so slowly, to the floor, he pocketed it, turned, and went out the door.

★

Hardball

Barbara D'Amato

W🌐RLDWIDE®

TORONTO • NEW YORK • LONDON • PARIS
AMSTERDAM • STOCKHOLM • HAMBURG
ATHENS • MILAN • TOKYO • SYDNEY

HARDBALL

A Worldwide Mystery/February 1991

This edition is reprinted by arrangement with Charles
Scribner's Sons, an imprint of Macmillan Publishing
Company.

ISBN 0-373-26066-0

Printed in U.S.A.

ONE

It was September, and the colors along the curve of Lake Michigan were ripening. Autumn is metallic here, chrome yellows on the locust trees, planted along the Outer Drive because they can stand the automobile-scented air, bronze oaks on the campus lawns, and brassy yellow maples near the administration buildings. The few trees that stayed green until the leaves fall take on the verdigris color of aged copper. I sometimes think even the concrete paths change color in the fall. They lose the sandy summer look of warmth and become a chilly brushed platinum, sueded but cold.

The University of Chicago lies on the curve at the southwest end of Lake Michigan. To the north it looks out across 350 miles of water. In winter, winds howl down from Canada across a frigid waste of floes and icebergs before they hit the shore. The water was already cooling. In another couple of months these tenacious trees would be sheathed in sleet.

The panorama lay outside the large windows of the reception hall. Inside, it was too warm.

The room was medium small and contained possibly fifteen to twenty people, loosely packed. Louise Sugarman and I sat on an uncomfortable sofa. The others were standing around holding glasses of sherry, each trying to convince his vis-à-vis of some pet point of view.

The babble of their voices surrounded me. A confetti of voices was in my left ear—people chattering and marking time before the start of the conference. Louise Sugarman's voice was in my right ear, agreeing to give me an interview. Her voice was the important one. This was a coup, and I was pleased with myself.

"On Monday, if that's all right," she said. "Early morning? Eight-thirty? I have a full day after ten. Maybe it's about time I gave an interview. I liked the piece you did on Billy Flowers."

Those sounds were the last I heard before the bomb blew.

There was a crack. No thunder, no echo, just a single loud crack. Louise Sugarman came hurtling toward me. She was distorted both by her speed and by something else that I had no time to understand. I must have lost a second or two then, because with no continuity I was lying on the floor. I was not unconscious. I just couldn't hear.

Other people froze facing us, their mouths big letter *O*'s. I saw sparkles of glass fall silently outward from the window that had been behind us. My head was bent forward against my chest. The back of my skull was jammed against a table leg. I looked down at my white silk turtleneck, which I had worn because I thought it made me appear dependable. Louise would trust me and give me an interview. The turtleneck was an odd color, grayish pink.

Half a dozen people loomed over me. I hadn't seen them come. I had not heard their footsteps. They were mouthing at me, but I couldn't hear their words. Everything was silent.

THE NEXT THING I knew, I could hear but not see. I tried opening my eyes, but it didn't make much difference. The room was dark. I could see the outline of a window. The sky outside was dark, which told me that hours had passed and it was night. There was a smell of antiseptic. An IV needle in my arm led to a tube that led to a plastic bag on a hook on a stand.

In the hall a masculine voice was saying, "The fact that a person *was* sleeping doesn't mean that a person is *still* sleeping."

A woman's voice said, "The doctor doesn't want her disturbed."

"I know that. I don't want her disturbed, either. But if you ask me, she's probably plenty disturbed as it is."

There was a disapproving silence.

"Tell you what," said the man's voice patiently. "I'll just look in. If Ms. Marsala has her eyes open, I'll go in. If not, I won't."

I'd identified the voice now. Capt. Harold McCoo, Chicago Police Department. Time to decide: close my eyes and pretend to sleep or leave them open?

I was bored. And very curious. I left them open and only blinked a little as the door let in light from the corridor. But when McCoo switched on the room light, I was blinded.

"Jeez, McCoo, warn a person before you do that."

"She's okay," McCoo said to the nurse as he shut the door in her face.

"What time is it?"

"Little bit past midnight. You've been sleeping ten hours."

"I don't remember being brought here."

He pulled over a chair and sat down. He was looking at my face and neck and hands. There were no bandages, so I figured the damage couldn't be too bad. No scars.

"You look like a bad sunburn," he said. I guess I was bruised, then.

He looked like a carving in chopped liver, but that's usual for him, so I didn't say it.

"What I need," he said, "is for you to tell me everything you saw before the device went off."

"'Device,' huh? Public service is getting to you. It was a bomb. What I saw—what I saw—I saw—"

I couldn't remember. I knew what he meant, but no picture came. It seemed for an instant I had it; then I lost it. My eyes filled with tears. How embarrassing!

"Catherine," he said, "what's the matter?"

"I don't know."

"Don't act like this. You're scaring me."

"I think they scrambled my brains."

"That's concussion."

"Give me a hint. What am I supposed to remember?"

"You were sitting next to Louise Sugarman on the sofa. There were people in the room, but not very close. On the other side of Louise Sugarman was a table. An end table. That's ironic enough, I guess."

"What?"

"Next to Louise—"

"I heard that part. Was anybody else hurt?"

"Other than Louise and you? No."

"Is that possible? To contain an explosion that closely?"

"Oh, sure. Progress in chemistry. Small gelignite explosions are almost surgically precise. A couple of people were cut by flying cocktail glass. It was quite a nicely calculated dev—bomb."

"What happened to Louise?"

He looked at me a second, probably wondering whether he should kid me along until I was better. But McCoo is a great believer in the healing power of reality, in which I wholeheartedly agree with him.

"She's dead."

He had a drink of my water, waiting to see how that would affect me. I felt fine, but for some reason a tear ran down one cheek.

"Aaah, M'cushla," he said.

"McCoo, don't *do* that. You may have an Irish-sounding name, but your ancestors came from somewhere in West Africa."

"East Africa," he said. "Why is it people know where everything is in Europe but nothing about Africa? Did I ever tell you how I got my first promotion?" He studied me out of the tail of his eye. "A lot of us, maybe a hundred and fifty, had taken the test, and, oh, fourteen or fifteen had passed high. There were five slots to be filled. So the captain, Sean Boyle his name was, he doesn't know us, but he's been sent the names to decide on who gets promoted. Those days, they did it that way. He goes down the list, and first he picks the three starting with Mc. McMahon, McCordle, and McCoo. Then he picks two others—it shouldn't look too Irish, you know? Next day he calls in the whole she-bang to give the glad news. Calls us up to meet him. I step up briskly and shake his hand. My! The look on that man's face!''

I smiled. He chortled. I said, "Okay. Okay. You've made me feel better now. Ask away.''

"The doctor did say mood swings were a possible effect of concussion.''

"Great.''

"Cat—''

"Let me ask one more thing first. Would the people who planted the bomb know that a person sitting next to Louise would only be injured? Not killed?''

"Well . . . Actually, I doubt it. Apparently they were willing to take that chance. But it didn't kill you.''

"Right.''

"Okay. Tell me what happened while you were sitting with Louise Sugarman. Did you see a cigarette package?''

"Was that what it was in?''

"Yeah.''

"I don't remember. What brand?''

"I don't want to put things in your mind. What about— Did anybody come near you two?''

"I don't know.''

"Christ, Cat, I've got a bomb going off in the same room as the chief of the DEA, an alderman, a state rep, the president of the northern Illinois PTA, and the head of Immigration and Naturalization, not to mention about a dozen various charity big shots and a handful of senior professors from three of the major schools. And nobody knows anything. You were the closest person. The closest living person. Think!''

I thought. Nothing came. Nothing clear. I saw Louise herself hurtling toward me, getting bigger and bigger. What went before that? What sofa? What table? Staring at the hospital ceiling, trying to picture that reception room, I saw only hospital ceiling. "She seemed very nice," I said, feeling inexpressibly sad. "I didn't expect to like her, but I liked her."

"All right. Don't try any more right now. I guess I shouldn't have asked. It'll come when the body and soul are ready for it."

"Will they ever be?"

"Yeah. And then," he said firmly, "you'll tell me everything."

"Okay."

"*Promise,* Cat?"

"Yes."

McCoo IS A GREAT deal more sympathetic than he wants to let on, but I knew he was serious—grimly serious—about telling him what I knew. No nonsense. I met him a few years ago when I did a profile on him for one of the major Chicago glossies. I don't write encomiums, and I thought it was straightforward, not a job of glorifying a public personality. For some reason, he was very happy with it. When I asked him why, he said, "Because there's enough bullshit in the world without me adding to it."

I took this to mean that the profile was honest. Pithy. To the point. He's an extremely professional person, McCoo is.

So I knew he really needed whatever I could remember. What was more important to me was that I wanted to remember, myself. I was hopping mad. For a person lying on her back, I was hopping mad. Mad enough that somebody had taken a chance on killing me. Furious that they had killed Louise Sugarman. I was seething.

TWO

IN ALL THE MYSTERY novels I read—and I read lots; they relax you at the end of a ghastly day the way nothing else does—the heroine or hero, badly injured, is always raring to get out of the hospital. Scarcely able to stand, he drags himself to the closet and pulls a shirt over his bandages.

Such was not my instinct. I had a headache, but that wasn't it. I was dizzy when I got up to walk to the bathroom, but that wasn't it, either.

It was breakfast in bed. When was the last time I had breakfast in bed? About the last time the Chicago City Council took a vote into which self-interest did not enter.

It came in on a tray held by a red-haired child, or perhaps a teenager; they're looking younger these days, now that I've entered my thirties. Since I had not been in the hospital the day before to place my order from the menu, they had included just about everything: scrambled eggs, pancakes, sliced peaches, orange juice, coffee, a plastic tub of syrup, a plastic container of butter, a plastic tub of cream, a paper envelope of pepper, two envelopes of salt, and two envelopes of sugar. I ate everything. I mean, this was an emergency, wasn't it? Getting one's strength back was paramount.

What came in right after breakfast also looked at first like a teenager and turned out to be my doctor.

"Feeling better?" he asked, his eyes resting pointedly on the denuded breakfast tray.

"Much. Thank you."

"Having a spot of retrograde amnesia?"

"I'm certainly having holes in my memory."

"For what happened before the accident or after the accident or more than that?"

"That wasn't any accident. I can't remember from just before the bomb went off, and some afterward, and I don't think I remember everything between the explosion and when I woke up last night, either."

"That's normal."

He did the things they do. Look in your eyes, flash their flashlight across your pupils, run wheels with pins up the soles of your foot, tap your knee.

"What day is this?" he asked.

"Sunday."

"How much is three plus one plus five?"

"Three hundred and fifteen."

"Ha. I can see your breakfast tasted fine," he said, "but how did it smell?"

"Splendid."

"Headache?"

"Some. Getting better since I had my coffee."

"Good. Dizziness? Anxiety?"

"Some dizziness. I thought the anxiety might be because somebody tried to blow me up."

He smiled. "I think that could be a contributing factor. Okay. You're doing pretty well. I want to keep you here today, but if nothing develops, you can leave tomorrow." He looked at me for an objection.

I said, "When do they serve lunch?"

ACTUALLY, I DIDN'T HAVE much to go home for right now. I'm not married. Never have been. I'm either skeptical of the institution or scared of it, depending on whether you're asking me or my mother. I live alone, at least most of the time, and my interview had died with Louise Sugarman. There are always a few future projects simmering on the back burner of the brain, but nothing lined up with definite appointments or that sort of thing. My article on the son of one of the Chicago judges jailed for corruption had just gone to the "Chicago Now" editor, who buys a lot of my stuff, so that had cleared the old desk. It would be a good piece when published, I thought. It had been triggered when I asked myself the question "How does it feel to grow up as the son of a judge—and become an attorney yourself—and then find your father hauled off to federal prison for extorting money from defendants?"

My parrot, named Long John Silver by his former owner, would be lonely. But with a clean cage, full water dish, and full feed hopper, he would be all right, even for two days. I allowed myself a modicum of praise for taking care of L.J.'s wants every morning first thing. It is the only housework I am at all responsible about.

One of the advantages of being a freelance is that no one is breathing down your neck to get the work done. It is also one of the disadvantages. Nobody pushes you. Nobody cares if you're not working, but if you don't work, you don't get paid.

Anyway, it was not time to work. It was time to think.

IT WAS NOW EXACTLY one year since the referendum to repeal the drug laws in the state of Michigan had narrowly failed. So narrowly that it was something like 1,200 votes in a state of over 9 million people.

This was the occasion of the conference at the University of Chicago. A year since the vote in the state of Michigan. Now a vote on a similar proposition was pending in Illinois. It would be on the same ballot as the gubernatorial election. There was a lot of pro-repeal feeling. The pro-repeal forces were led by Louise Sugarman.

Michigan had flirted with repeal for a very simple reason. The state was virtually bankrupt. Squeezed by rising school costs, prison costs, welfare costs, highway costs, state police costs, court costs, pollution cleanup costs—I could go on, but why?—and losing revenue because of the declining auto and chemical industries, the state found there was no money left. The shortfall was larger every year.

Somebody in Lansing had an idea. Revoke the laws criminalizing drugs. Suddenly the costs of enforcement vanish. Millions of dollars going into the Department of Corrections, the Michigan State Police, municipal law enforcement, and all kinds of related services become available for other uses. Wow.

It is easy to imagine the fire storm of protest at the idea. Shock. Horror. Unthinkable.

Repeal sounded dangerous to me, and I like new ideas as a rule. I lined up pretty much with everybody else. Drugs are one of the plagues of modern times. It's putting a thief in your mouth to steal away your brains—and then some. Sometimes your brains never came back to you.

Church groups mobilized. PTAs issued warnings. Police chiefs issued warnings. An organization composed entirely of high school principals formed to combat the idea.

But—when the state honcho who had suggested it threw in the suggestion that 50 percent of the money saved could be earmarked for drug-treatment programs, there was a lot of stopping and thinking. Another character pointed out that they would put thirty-four times as much money into drug rehab as was presently being spent. And if 10 percent of what was being spent on keeping drug offenders in prison was spent instead on education programs at the grade-school level, then the education programs would increase a hundred times—well! The proposal that at first appeared idiotic garnered very nearly 50 percent of the votes.

And probably the reason it did not do just a little better was that there was no charismatic individual leading the movement. There was no attractive person for the idea to crystallize around.

Illinois, however, had just such a person. Warm, pretty, grandmotherly Louise Sugarman. She was a little bit plump, not at all glamorous, not very tall. She was soft-spoken. She wore soft, pretty clothes, like loose angora sweaters, and her white hair was softly curled. She was pleasant and courteous. Her reform group was called Common Sense. Nobody could look more commonsensical than Louise Sugarman. Single-handedly, she made the whole movement completely credible.

Can anyone be surprised that thousands of people regarded her as anathema, practically the Antichrist?

And sure as hell there were some heavy interest groups out there whose cash flow would be guillotined if she got her way.

THREE

IN ILLINOIS, LOUISE SUGARMAN and her repeal movement had become the most interesting thing in years, even more interesting than the revelations about the senator who kept a hundred thousand dollars in medium-sized bills in shoe boxes in his secretary's closet. And claimed he didn't take bribes. To newspapers, television talk-show hosts, and magazines, Louise was the *dernier cri,* the bee's knees. I mean, we're talking serious fascination here.

And she gave out *very* few personal interviews. She and her group willingly answered questions about the issues. They published booklets. They joined symposia on pro and con of repeal. She spoke at PTAs, WCTUs, ACLUs, AAUPs, the AMA. But she practically never would answer personal questions. Personal interviews—graphically called profiles in the media biz, being largely two-dimensional—were not for Louise Sugarman.

I have to admit, I didn't believe she could be as Goody Twoshoes as she sounded. Here she was indirectly pushing substances that stole sense and jobs and families and lives. My reportorial instincts were up: What was in it for her? What buried resentments might cause her to want revenge on society?

I don't do exposés. The kind where irrelevant dirty linen of some public figure is washed by the reporter to make a big splash. But I *do* do character study. I wanted to watch her closely and make up my own mind.

Damn if I didn't like her. She was unassuming and spoke English as I like to hear it—clear, unemotional, to the point.

And her last words, spoken to me, were, "Maybe it's about time I gave an interview. I liked the piece you did on Billy Flowers."

Billy Flowers was a cop who had been shot and paralyzed when his partner raised his gun, hit a felony suspect, a suspected drug pusher, on the head with the gun butt and the gun discharged, striking Flowers and severing his spinal cord just above the kidneys. What made it remarkable were three things: First, the suspect had not been resisting arrest. Second, Flowers had warned his captain repeatedly that his partner was a hothead, likely to injure a citizen and get the cops in trouble. Third, Flowers, in a wheelchair, testified for the defense at the trial of the suspected pusher. That was what made the case remarkable. What made Flowers remarkable was that he did not hold a grudge against his partner. He understood the stresses the man faced, and he understood that not everybody had the same resistance to the same stresses. He just thought the man shouldn't be a cop. What Sugarman liked about the piece, I'm not sure. I wasn't about to argue with a coup in hand. Almost in hand.

But if I had not been able to go to the University of Chicago symposium and meet her, Sugarman would never have sought me out for an interview, that's for sure. I got into the sherry party by pulling strings. Namely, my uncle Ben, who was head of Parents Against Substance Abuse.

To get a story, would I use my relatives? You bet I would.

But then, they use me, too. Sitting in the barber's chair, they pick up a *Chicago* magazine and say, "Look, Manny. Here's my little niece Catherine with an article on the fire department."

I had approached Uncle Ben the minute I saw he was on the University of Chicago panel with Louise Sugarman.

Ben Hoskinson, strictly speaking, was not an uncle. He was my aunt's first cousin. There are probably societies with such a consuming interest in genealogies that they have a name for that kind of relationship. But I called him Uncle

Ben rather than Cousin Ben mainly because he was a generation older than I.

Parents Against Substance Abuse is usually called PASA, giving rise to *que pasa?* remarks. Uncle Ben is its chairman.

I went to his office to see him face-to-face. Rule 6B in interviewing: Go face-to-face if you possibly can, especially if it's something the other guy may not want to talk about or do for you. It's harder to turn down a person face-to-face than on the telephone.

"Why would you *want* to meet Louise?" Uncle Ben asked.

"So that I can talk with her face-to-face. That's why."

"She doesn't give interviews during speaking engagements."

"I'm just going to ask her for an appointment later."

"Why not call her?"

"I'd get a secretary. It's harder for people to turn you down face-to-face."

"Why Sugarman, Catherine? She's a terrible person. Well, not a terrible person, *personally,* but she doesn't understand what a terrible thing she's doing."

"She's news, Uncle Ben."

"She doesn't give interviews, anyhow."

"Maybe that's why she's news."

"You want to interview somebody, Catherine, why not interview me?"

What a thing to say! For all I knew, maybe he'd been feeling left out and working up to this for years. I looked at Uncle Ben with new eyes. He was a gentle sort of guy. About fifty-five, he was the sort of man who carried his head like a stone. It was too heavy for his neck. It kept sinking down to mid-shoulder level. Then, after a while, he'd remember and straighten up, and then the whole sinking process would start again. I didn't want to hurt him.

"I can't interview you, Uncle Ben. It would look like nepotism. Or uncleism. It wouldn't look right."

"Oh, so that's it."

He seemed satisfied.

"Listen, you can take a guest to the sherry reception, can't you? Any organization always lets the speakers bring their significant others."

"Yes, I suppose so."

"Is Aunt Elise going with you?" They were both members of the PASA, but I knew they didn't go everywhere together.

"No, she has a PTA lecture." He was turning it over in his mind. This was the time not to interrupt. I waited. After half a minute he brightened.

"Why not? That's not a bad idea, really."

"Shall I meet you there, or shall we drive together?"

Rule 11: strike while the iron is hot.

"Better meet you, Catherine. If you decide to talk with her afterward, or some such thing, I'll want to leave. I have nothing to say to that woman."

So I WENT TO THE symposium. As I lay in bed thinking of it, trying to remember, the first part was perfectly clear. Walking up to the auditorium, sweeping my feet through dry copper-colored leaves on the sidewalk. I even remembered the rustling, the sound of fall.

Hundreds of people were streaming into the hall, though it was half an hour before the program was supposed to start. Some looked like potential hecklers, angry, with little slit mouths. Some were students. Some were aging hippies in Levi's and with silver threads in their beards. Several wore white buttons with a green marijuana leaf rampant and the slogan "Let a thousand flowers bloom." You'd have thought it was 1968 again. Was that more than twenty years ago! Gawd!

There was a banner from a recent event in Wisconsin. A marijuana festival had actually been planned and scheduled. Wisconsin marijuana growers and assorted fans had set an autumn rally, just like apple growers. Then the authorities banned it, and it faded from the media.

I detoured around past the auditorium entrance to the back of the building, where I was supposed to enter through a door marked Authorized Personnel Only. It led to a cinder-block corridor. When the cinder-block corridor changed to a walnut-panelled hall and my way was blocked by a security guard, I knew I was in the right place.

"Name?"

"Catherine Marsala."

"Okay," said Mr. Clipboard. "First turn to your right, then straight ahead. You'll hear the reception before you see it."

"Thanks."

I left him making a line through my name.

Just inside the reception-room door, one of those moments happened. The kind of moment when you look at a crowd, just scanning, and you catch somebody's eye. He was a sleek young man. Rather young, at least; say, thirty-five. That put him in what I considered my possibles range. He smiled. He started toward me. He was slender and very neatly dressed in a dark gray pinstripe suit. I smiled.

Then someone behind him called, "Charles!"

He turned to look, nodded, turned back to me. He made that "see you later" gesture with a raised index finger and went to talk with whoever had called him.

You want babble, go to a university presymposium party. Lots of articulate people in a small space, like molecules in compressed, hot gas. Of the fifteen or twenty people, I knew several. My Uncle Ben, of course—dipping his heavy head into his sherry glass for a sip, then pulling back up. His assistant, Torkel Gates, was leaning over a plump woman in a pink flowered dress and gesturing enthusiastically. Torkel is a blond-blond-blond man with pale eyelashes and pinkish eyes, and the ends of everything on his face are red. Red earlobes, red nose tip, red chin. Even his brow ridge under

he transparent eyebrows is red and rubbed looking, as if
someone had struck him lightly.

Uncle Ben was going to be one of the speakers in what was
planned as a debate. He stared around the room, and I
thought he anticipated some tough argument, because he
said, "Catherine, I hope you're not going to fall for any of
he arguments these people dish out."

"Uncle Ben, I'm an adult."

"Mmmp."

"I can listen to arguments and make up my own mind. I
interview some very persuasive people, and I don't buy
everything they say."

"Some of their arguments are superficially plausible."

"And you know—there's Teddy to think about." Teddy
was my youngest brother. And Teddy seemed to me a living
reason to keep drugs illegal.

"Oh, right. I wasn't thinking."

"That's okay."

"They really shouldn't give them a forum like this."

"Well, then, why are you dignifying it by being here and
speaking at it?"

"Because otherwise they'd do it without me."

There were a couple of eminent professors, of course, and
a sprinkling of three-piece-suit sorts. And one with black
shiny shoes, navy-blue polyester pants, light blue shirt, dark
tie, et cetera. That is the uniform of the nonuniformed cop.

It was Lt. Stan Gotchka, the head of the narco division of
the Chicago Police Department. And head of the class. He
is six feet six. His bristly, brush-cut cranium stood out above
all the rest.

Stan was across half a room, and I am under five feet two,
so when I'm in a crowd, I tend to vanish. But I stuck my
right arm up and waggled the fingers to get his attention.
"Yo! Stan!"

He saw me, which only illustrates how tall the fellow is.
Somebody pushed a tray of sherry at me. I took one. By the

time I looked up from a sip, there was six and a half feet of cop.

"Going to give a speech today, Stan, or are you just lending authority?"

"I'm doing fifteen minutes on the organization of the city narcotics squad. Factual."

"No sales pitch?"

"I'm not political."

"Okay." A hand appeared with a round tray of mysteries on toast. Stan and I each took one.

"Mmm. Olive spread," Stan said. "Not too bad."

"I thought it was anchovy paste."

"Could be that, too."

"What's the program?"

He pushed a sheet of thick creamy paper at me. There is a weed in the back of my brain that my mother planted. It looked at the program card and said Not Engraved. The up-to-date part of me admired the clarity of the laser printing. The speakers in order of appearance were Leota Parks of the northern Illinois PTA, Dr. Cameron Lloyd of Bennett Medical School, Lt. Stanley Gotchka, head of the Chicago Police Department's drug enforcement section, Professor Robert Q. Erdmann of Lehigh College, Glen Barton of the Drug Enforcement Administration, Ben Hoskinson, president of Parents Against Substance Abuse, and Louise Sugarman, president of Common Sense.

"We were told we'd get fifteen minutes each," Stan said.

"Seven speakers. That's a long program."

"Four of them do an hour. Then we break for coffee. Then three speak. Then questions."

"Nice and tidy. But no University of Chicago professors."

"Oh, you know. They like to appear eclectic."

"Do cops know words like eclectic?"

"It's part of the exam. If you know the right words, you get promoted lieutenant."

"You should be ashamed of yourself," spat a voice behind me. I mean, spat. There was a splattery quality to the *S*'s. I swung around, thinking I was being attacked, but the woman in the flowered pink dress was hulking over a pleasant grandmotherly-looking woman in a honey-colored suit. Louise Sugarman was the one in the suit. She was saying seriously, "Let's just talk about the issues, Leota."

"Children are the issue. Your children will suffer. Your— You have grandchildren, haven't you? Do you want pushers to have a free shot at them? What kind of a woman are you?" The large pink one was wearing a chain necklace with a pendant that looked like a totem pole. It swayed in counterpoint to her head movements.

"Leota, I'm trying to solve the pusher problem. We've created—"

"You are a disgrace! Do you want cocaine sold at every candy counter? Is somebody paying you—"

"Leota, we've created a pusher class in this country. We've made—"

"And I would think a woman would be more sympathetic!"

"We've made pushing pay very well."

"Shut up! Just shut up!" the woman said, and she stalked away.

"Who's the pink menace?" I asked Stan.

"Leota Parks, chair of the northern Illinois PTA."

Louise Sugarman must have heard me. "Sorry about that," she said.

"It hardly seemed to be *your* fault."

"She's got every right to express her opinion. I just shouldn't get into personal conversation with her. She's much more controlled behind a lectern."

"Speaking of personal conversations—" I said.

She smiled and cocked her head. Just as my grandmother used to when I was going to ask for a quarter to go to the store.

"My name is Catherine Marsala. I'm a freelance writer."

"I've seen your name."

Friend for life. Stan had discreetly moved away. I reminded myself to seek him out and thank him later.

"I've always wanted to do a piece on you," I said.

"A personal piece?"

"Um, yes."

"Well, you see how it is. The less they know about me, the better."

"You think you'd be attacked more, the more people knew about you?"

"Not more, but more personally."

"And?"

"And I'd like to focus on issues. I'd like people to try to be reasonable."

"But—"

"Maybe we could go sit down over there."

"Great!" I said. She and I pushed through a crowd, cradling our sherry glasses, toward a long burlap-covered sofa against the wall. There was a table at the end of the sofa. An end table.

Zaaap!

Memory quit on me.

In my mind I could not see us getting to the sofa or sitting down. My mental film strip jumped forward a hundred or more frames. She was sitting next to me, closer to the table than I was, saying, "Maybe it's about time..." She was thinking as she spoke. "I liked the piece you did on Billy Flowers."

I liked her. Now, I'm as susceptible to flattery as the next person, but that wasn't why I liked her. My guess was she liked that piece for the right reasons.

I liked her attitude. Not her views, necessarily. I stood firmly in the camp that thought repeal of the drug laws was dangerous. But personally I can accept differences of opinion as long as people are willing to discuss why they believe what they believe without bullying me and without trying to fog up the issue with truisms, mawkishness, and recourse to whimpering in its many forms. As McCoo had said, there is enough bullshit in the world, and Louise Sugarman seemed to be one of the people who didn't want to add to it.

Zaap! A crack and she's hurtling toward me.

Zaap! Another frame jump and I'm on the floor, jammed up against the leg of a chair. People are making *O*'s of their mouths.

Zaap! And McCoo is at the hospital, demanding to talk with me.

Nothing in between. It was eerie. It was more than eerie; it was terrifying. I felt as if someone had come along and scooped out part of my brain.

How long had we sat on the sofa?

Had anybody approached us?

Who was nearby?

I lay there in bed trying to recover lost images. Nothing worked. Thinking as hard as I could, picturing closely, in minute detail, right up to the moment of the blackout—that didn't work. Nothing. Drop-off. Fall off the end of the world and be eaten by dragons.

I tried sneaking up on it. Went to the bathroom, came out, drank some water, thinking slyly about the weather or the Bears. Then a quick mental turn to try to catch the memory peeking around the corner behind me.

No go.

THE NEXT MORNING, well before cockcrow, my youthful neurologist returned. He had a few harder questions for me, like adding twenty-four and seventeen and who was the vice-president of the United States. While I had trouble with the second, I must have done genius work on the batch as a whole, because he said that after breakfast I could go.

"I want my memory back."

"It'll come. Probably."

"What does probably mean? How likely? Fifty-fifty? Ninety percent?"

"Well, in your case, I'd guess over eighty percent. Don't worry and don't try to force it. It won't help."

Don't worry? He just didn't understand. I didn't know what had happened, and I couldn't tell whether there was somebody out in crazyland who maybe thought I knew more than I did and wanted to get me. But one thing he was right about. A sleepless night had convinced me that trying to force it was no good.

Breakfast came.

I was just starting vigorous pancake and syrup and butter action when the door burst open.

My dear friend, Mike Murphy, red and enraged, yelled, "All right, Cat! Why didn't you call and tell me?" Mike is very sexy, and sexiest when he's angry.

"Tell you what?"

"You're in the hospital. You're hurt. You don't call. What are you trying to prove?"

"I'm not hurt. Look at me. I've been kept around for observation, sort of."

At the "sort of" he actually sneered. People don't sneer a lot these days. I've heard it was a major skill during the Elizabethan era. But he does it well.

"Then why are you purplish and bluish and—"

"Bruises. You surely don't want me to call you every time I get a bruise?"

"You are so frustrating. Here's a rose."

"Thank you." It was pink and tiny and lovely. I felt tears in my eyes again. Emotional liability. Always a problem with these head injuries. "Have some coffee," I said. "I've got plenty."

"Oh, all right." There was a Styrofoam cup in the bathroom. He poured his coffee. I ate a sausage.

"There was no answer at your apartment," he said. "Don't you expect me to worry?"

"How'd you find out where I was?"

"Newspapers. It's major news. The blast was big headlines all over Chicago. Downstate. New York to San Fran. Also the networks."

"'Louise Sugarman Killed.' That would be all the news they wanted. So how'd you know I was—?"

"Last paragraph in the *Trib*. 'Also injured in the blast was Catherine Marsala, a reporter. Marsala was reported in good condition in Wesley Memorial Hospital.'"

"'A reporter.' Hmmp."

"*The* reporter, they should have said."

"The *writer*!"

"Oh, very well. Listen, Cat. I have to go out to the Mississippi River for two days. I'll be back Wednesday. Will you be all right?"

"Sure. Will *you* be all right?"

He sat up. "Of course I will."

"While you're there, Mike, try not—"

"I know all about it." He got up very fast. "I'll call you." And he was out the door.

Damn it! I ought to know better.

I could bite my tongue sometimes. But being me, I finished all the pancakes instead. I mean, I know a crisis when I see one.

The paper napkin was just proving it could not remove syrup from fingers when I had another visitor. John Banks. He walked into the room carrying a large brown paper bag, wearing a lightweight navy wool topcoat over a three-piece suit, and looking, as always, solid and respectable.

"Catherine," he said, "you should not do these things."

Then he kissed me lightly. A second time more firmly.

"I didn't do anything. I was just sitting there asking for an interview. Wondering if anyone was going to drop a bomb in the conversation."

"I'm certain you did something."

"To bring it on myself?" We both smiled. It was an old argument. He hefted the brown paper bag, and at the same moment his eye caught sight of the little pink rose on the bed table. He glanced at the door and back at the rose. He raised the paper bag a couple of inches farther. There was no need to read minds. He knew it was Michael's rose, and he wanted to put his bag down on top of it.

And he decided not to.

"Here." He put the bag on the bed. "They said you're being discharged. I'll drive you home."

"Okay. What's this?"

"A set of clothes from your apartment. I gave Long John Silver more water. He bit me."

"How'd you get in?"

"I used all of my persuasive powers on the super. Also, he'd seen the item in the *Trib*."

"But I have clothes here somewhere." I had been hanging out in those natty things they gave you in hospitals. Mine was flannel with blue dots. And over it one of those things they call gowns but have no back.

All he said was "I'll wait in the visitors' lounge while you change and pack."

I put on the pants and sweatshirt he had brought. The dozen or so pencils and pens I always carry were in the metal nightstand and I slipped them in the pants pockets, as I always do. Ditto notepad. My suede boots, ivory to go with the fancy stuff I had worn to the symposium, were on the floor, and I stepped into them. The rose Mike had brought I pinned onto the shoulder of the sweatshirt. Then I went to the closet to put my good clothes from the interview into the bag.

The white silk shirt and ivory skirt were stuck to each other. When I pulled them off the hanger, they were as rigid as cardboard. I looked closer. They were splattered with Louise Sugarman's blood and brains.

FOUR

THE APARTMENT LOOKED like utopia. Maybe these people who rush to leave their hospital beds aren't so dumb. I guess it was mainly that I was getting tired of strangers walking in on me to draw blood or pump up a blood-pressure cuff or take my temperature. Of course, my apartment came without breakfast in bed, but I'd worry about that later.

John went to LJ's cage and let him out. He swooped over to me and perched on my shoulder. People tell me that birds are not affectionate. These people are wrong. LJ had missed me.

LJ said, *"Aawwwk!"* He talks, but only when he wants to.

John put the brown paper bag in the closet. Then he picked it up again. My yukky clothes were in it.

"I think I'll just drop this off at the cleaners," he said.

"It's Sunday."

"So it is. I'll leave it in my car and drop it off tomorrow."

Dear John. Dear, unromantic John. He had anticipated my clotted clothing just from reading the news story and had gone ahead to my apartment to get me fresh.

One gentleman caller who brings roses, one who brings what you need. Gee.

It was nearly noon. He said, "Or then again, I could stay with you," he said.

"No, you have things to do. And I'm okay."

"You're not going to start rushing around—"

"Hey, John. They let me out because I was ready to be let out."

"That doesn't mean you should start rushing around."

"I'll be good."

He didn't believe it. "Take a nap."

"John, really—"

"No, never mind. I will rely on your common sense." He smiled broadly, leaving me to draw my own conclusions about whether he was being sarcastic or not. "But at precisely six o'clock pip emma I will be back. You and I will go to mother's for dinner."

"*Awwk!*" I sounded like LJ.

"She's not that bad."

"She's not bad at all. She's just different from me."

"She has Lucinda back."

Lucinda was the cook. Lucinda and John's mother had had a tiff. Apparently the tiff was over.

"Oh?"

"And Lucinda's making chicken baked in cream, and pecan pie."

"Oh!"

"Six o'clock."

He walked out the door, and he didn't forget the paper bag, either. He knew he had the last word.

Only he didn't. I ran to the front of the so-called living room, where the apartment overlooks the street, and threw the window up. I held LJ so he wouldn't fly out. John was just emerging from the front door, striding rapidly.

"If you hurry," I yelled, "you can pick up some pecans and cream for Lucinda. Otherwise, when you tell her she's got to make pecan pie, she's going to snatch you bald headed!"

I FELT A TUG ON MY shoulder. I looked down and saw LJ eating my rose. "Idiot bird!" I said, shooing him off. He flew to the curtain rod in the living room, where he shook his feathers. Then he turned around, fixed me with a reptilian eye, and squawked, "Prophet! *Braak!* Thing of evil!! *Braaak!*"

Long John Silver's former owner had been an English professor.

Bird fanciers will tell you that polly doesn't want a cracker. Polly would prefer a peanut or a rose. What I wondered was this: When John let LJ out of the cage, did he know that parrots liked to eat flowers?

THE COMMON SENSE headquarters was in what might be called the outer loop, not quite the high-rent district but close enough so movers and shakers could get there without a freeway trip. There were posters on its modest storefront window. I was betting on people being there, even though it was Sunday. After all, they had a crisis on their hands. And sure enough, the lights were on inside. Apparently life went on without Louise Sugarman.

I was wearing my Earnest outfit; the importance of being earnest in this case was to look like a real, legit volunteer. This involved a dark suit, a little bit too long, and a tweedy jacket. No makeup. Glasses with thin pinkish plastic rims. I had been able to get into these clothes within four minutes of John's departure, when he was well out of sight. The bruises were more difficult. They were turning a moldy yellow now. I left them as is.

I was coding myself as Not a Reporter. Reporters are trendily dressed, as a rule. They never know when they might be on camera.

"Good afternoon!" said the young man at the desk.

"Good morning." I sat down in the chair next to the desk. Rule 15 of reporting: Get at their eye level to get their confidence.

"Oh, right. What can I do for you?"

"I want to help the campaign."

"Do you mean a donation, or do you want to work for us? We can use either one." He smiled.

"Well, I have a donation to make." I pulled out two crumpled five-dollar bills. "But I was thinking of work. I have more time than money."

That was true. And more's the pity, I had precious little time.

"And I thought"—I hesitated—"maybe you'd need extra help, you know, right *now*."

"You mean because of Louise."

"Yes." Rule 16 of reporting: Unless you just want them to repeat what you've said, don't prime the pump. Let them come up with whatever is on top of their minds.

"Well, it's been a bitch of a body blow, I can tell you that."

I wanted to ask why but waited.

"I realize," he said, warming indignantly, "that everybody thinks she was such a great figurehead. You know, grandmotherly and all that—"

Aha! Dirt! This was what I was here for. The poop on the real Louise Sugarman. Somebody gets killed, you have a right to ask whether somebody didn't like her.

"—but that wasn't the half of it. She was a *thinker*. She was the one who analyzed what the drug laws cost the state. She pulled the percentages out of the state budget. She came up with most of our slogans. She wrote brochures. I mean, she was no figurehead; she was always here working."

"Sort of a slave driver?"

He looked at me as if I were a lunatic.

"She was a"—he worked hard on the word for a minute; then his eyes lit up—"a darling," he said.

"Oh! Sorry!"

"Well, you didn't know her. Say, pardon me for asking, but what happened to your face?"

"I was in an accident."

"Mmm. I had one last year. My fault, really, too. I was tailgating a taxi. I was in the hospital three days, and Louise came every evening with my favorite food. Because the hospital food was *yechhh*."

"What's your favorite food?"

"Popeye's fried chicken with honey and biscuits."

Visions of a sticky hospital bed covered with bones competed with visions of saintly Louise Sugarman. I said, "If I came in when I get a chance—to a certain extent, I can schedule my own time—I could help with mailing. Folding. Stuffing. Stamping?"

"Sure. If you want to do that, always come after one P.M. Our printer delivers at noon. But we don't do mailings every day."

"I'll take my chances," I said.

The street door behind me opened, ringing a bell. My new friend said, "Hi, Mandy. How's it going?"

Mandy was a young woman carrying a white paper bag with golden arches printed on it. She broke stride a second, said, "Ter-er-erible," on a rising note, burst into tears, and ran for the back room.

"Louise's secretary," my friend said.

Dreams of finding in-house enemies of Louise Sugarman faded and died.

I HADN'T STOPPED trying to remember what had happened just before the bomb went off. But I had come to think the doctor was right. Don't chase it. Let it come to you.

So I dressed in something John's mother would approve of. Translation: not Levi's. And even bought a bottle of a gluey substance called Cover-Up that was said to be good for blemishes. Since my face and body were one big blemish, I considered bathing in it. Rejected that. Dabbed it on the worst places on my face and hoped it looked natural.

LORD! I LOVE CHICAGO! It's got everything.

The Banks place was a *pile*. Giant dark gray granite blocks the size of Toyotas made up the walls and squeezed the windows into slits. But it was a narrow pile. It sat on a narrow lot a couple of blocks from the lake, surrounded by other piles that loomed close to it. It was four stories tall, not counting the basement.

Judging from the interior darkness, I hoped I never found out what the basement looked like.

Chandeliers fought the gloom of high ceilings and dark wood. Mrs. Banks swooped toward us over oak parquet. "Catherine, dear!" she said, and she managed to sound perfectly delighted.

"Mrs. Banks. It's nice of you to have me on such short notice."

She smiled the trouble-free smile of the woman who has a cook.

"Come in here, dear. Ward is in the living room."

Ward is Mr. Banks. He and John have a very cautious relationship. Someday I'm going to find out why.

"Here are John and Catherine!" she called to Ward as we entered the living room. Ward swung around and said, "Aah-mm. Good t'see you, mm-umm." I don't think he knew who I was, in spite of his wife's prompting. He pushed a highball glass back on the sideboard and started splashing stuff into a tray of glasses. Mumbling, "Drink, mm-mm?"

He swung back to us, a glass in each hand. One for me and one for Mrs. Banks. Ladies first. "Sherry, hum-mm?" he said.

I sipped as he turned and took up the other two glasses, for himself and John.

Sipped the sherry, smelled it fragrance—and *zzaaap!*

I was in the reception room at the University of Chicago, taking a sip of sherry. Louise Sugarman sat next to me. Her face was turned toward me and she was saying, "Maybe it's about time I gave an interview—"

The room was a picture with good focus in the center and fuzzy edges.

I saw a big pink blob, Leota Parks, for sure, in her flowered dress. I saw Lt. Stan Gotchka more clearly. He had a drink in one hand; the other hand held a cigarette to his chest. Torkel Gates was fiddling with something on the table that looked like bread sticks on a tray. One of the eminent professors, probably Erdmann, was gesturing emphatically with his big red pen. Another of the eminent professors, probably Dr. Lloyd, was slouched in a chair near the windows. He held a roll of paper, notes, I supposed, for the talk he was going to give. He was chewing pensively on the edge of the roll. Uncle Ben was listening patiently to a woman wearing lavender, whom I saw from the back, and he seemed to be contemplating blowing cigar smoke in her face. Behind these people were others I could not see.

A young man with a tray of sherry was approaching us. A young woman with a tray of either olive spread or anchovy munchies was walking away from us. Student help.

The sense of horror I felt at that instant was probably not anything I had felt at the time.

"—liked the piece you did on Billy Flowers."

I heard the crack again. Sherry glasses slid slowly and soundless off the young man's tray, somersaulting to the floor. Munchies flew up into the air. Louise Sugarman blew up. She blew toward me, becoming huge, crashing into me. Now I knew—most of my bruises had not been caused by the blast, exactly, but by being struck by Louise's body.

At the impact, I turned sideways, slightly away from her. Painlessly sailing through the air, I could see everybody at the other side of the room. The side I had not been watching before. As I floated gently down, I saw the exit door. There was a red Exit sign over it.

The sleek young man stood there with a small black box in his hand. As I sank, oh, so slowly, to the floor, he pocketed it, turned, and went out the door.

FIVE

WELL, ENOUGH OF THIS lollygagging around at dinner parties and hospitals. Back to work.

Monday at the crack of noon I hopped out of bed to get straight to work, sat down again and took two aspirin from the bottle on the nightstand, waited fifteen minutes lying flat on my back, and hopped up to get to work.

I made a list of whom I had to see. McCoo was on it, but toward the bottom. I had given him my promise. I would tell him what I remembered, but I hadn't said I'd do it immediately.

Maybe tomorrow.

Today I had serious work to do. Interviews don't come to you. You go to them.

John had been wonderful the night before at his parents' house. I had come a hairbreadth from fainting away over the sherry. He saw that and sat me down. I mumbled something like "Awfully tricky, these head injuries."

Then I sat on their chaise longue for quite a long time, but not because I could not safely move. The dizziness only lasted a few seconds, but I was trying to retain every single detail of that twenty-second flash that had come back to me. Losing it again would be a tragedy. And since I had remembered it visually, like a photo, I thought I also had to convert it to words in my head for permanence. It had been several days since I trusted my memory.

I looked at it and repeated what I saw over and over to myself.

Then John and his parents and I went into their large brocade-stuffed dining room and had dinner. Including the chicken and the pecan pie. I ate with what my mother would call "a healthy appetite." After all, a crisis is a crisis.

John brought me home. Stayed in case I should get sick during the night. Slept on the sofa, a perfect gentleman. Left for work without waking me. Wow.

ONE CUP OF COFFEE cleared a brain fog I hadn't realized I was suffering from. Panic set in. I charged frantically across the living room to the phone, tripped on a sofa pillow but didn't fall, and rang Bernie at the *Trib*.

"Bernie! Quick! Is the Sugarman funeral today?"

"Good morning, Cat. I'm glad to hear your voice, too."

"Bernie! Please!"

"Yes, it is."

"Where?"

"St. Ed's. Then Rosehill."

"When?"

"At—mmm, in thirty-five minutes. Say, Cat, this is great! You've just about mastered four of the reporter's basic five. Where, When, What, and Who. When you master Why, maybe we can hire you at the *Trib*."

"Never. You're too bossy."

"I can be cajoled."

"And I'm not good at taking orders."

"You can say that again."

"Listen, I'll butter you up later. Thanks. 'Bye."

Cat Marsala, a costume for all occasions. Quick—into something black. I can't pretend it was difficult. When you grow up in an Italian family, you *always* own something black.

Cat Marsala, lightning-change artist. Also, ace taxi hailer and backseat driver.

THE SERVICE HAD started, but that was all right. I slipped into the back. Found Uncle Ben next to me. He wore a wool coat smelling of mothballs. It was autumn, but the day wasn't cold. I suppose he'd taken the coat out to air in preparation for winter.

"What are you doing here?" I whispered at him. "You hated the woman."

"I do not hate people," he said softly.

"Intense dislike?"

"I think she was sincere. She was just *wrong*. I'm here to show respect for her sincerity."

And then maybe he was here in case news photographers showed up.

Max Sugarman, Louise's husband, was Jewish, but his wife had been born Catholic. St. Edmund's was Catholic. They were not holding the longest possible funeral mass. Maybe they were trying to make it easy on reporters. Of which there were at least thirty.

Soon we were milling about on a side terrace in the sun. I circulated as much as possible, hoping to have a flash of insight the instant I set eyes on the killer.

Max Sugarman was there, of course. I would have to talk with him, but not today. People were filing past him, and I joined the line.

"I'm so sorry," I told him.

He looked at me with rather vague eyes, started to say, "Thank you—" then did a double take. "You were hurt with her. When she was—hurt."

"Yes."

"You look well recovered. Oh, dear. I should have called you."

"Oh, no—"

"It's such a shame. They were aiming for her. I'm sorry you were caught in it."

He was a good-looking man in his sixties. Very thin.

"I'm sorry *she* was caught in it."

"Well, she had a great many enemies. It wasn't just a matter of people disagreeing with her. There were people who loathed her for what she believed."

"She seemed a very sweet person. She had just told me she would give me an interview."

"Really?"

"Well, I'd better move along. You have people waiting to talk with you."

I walked a couple of feet farther on, having planted the seeds. It would be important to interview him soon. Husbands sometimes do kill their wives, after all, and even if he was pure as snow, he still knew more than anyone else about who Louise's enemies had been. But, much as I wanted the story, I didn't have the heart to push in on him while his bereavement was new and raw.

Turning toward the thickest part of the crowd, I saw Torkel, Uncle Ben's aide. And Stan Gotchka, the tall cop. And the two professors, Lloyd and Erdmann, whom I was going to have to learn to tell apart. Not Leota Parks, the PTA lady. Except for her, it was old home week. One almost wanted to look around for bombs.

I looked around.

There was the sleek young man.

"Hi!" I said.

He smiled lazily. "For a person who was blown up," he said, "you don't look bad at all."

"It's all done with Max Factor."

More soberly, he said, "How badly were you hurt?"

"Bruises. A soupçon of concussion."

"I suppose I should have rushed to your side. But everybody was lending a hand."

"I don't know. I seem to have been out cold."

"The paramedics were there in minutes."

"I don't remember that, either." Clearly, he did not know that I knew he had left before the paramedics could even have been called. Ace in the hole for me. "Did the police come?" I asked.

"Are you kidding? What do you think?"

"I think the police came."

"Swarmed. Say, how do you feel about graveside cere-
monies and things like pushing the dirt in on top of roses
and such?"

"I'm extremely negative about them."

"Let's go have a drink instead."

"You bet."

BONEY'S WAS DARK oak, "lite" beer, and lots of booths.
Privacy. My teenybopper neurologist had said not to drink,
so I ordered lite beer. It was execrable. It would keep me
from drinking. The human mind was a wondrous tool. He
had red wine. It should have told me something.

"Who are you?" I asked.

"You don't know?" He looked at me suspiciously. "I
don't mean that you should, necessarily. It's just that some
people do." He must have been convinced by my blank face.
"I'm Charles Jaffee."

"Aha!"

"Gee—a direct hit."

"I know your father. Met him at a Cook County func-
tion a while back." A pink tea. A political bun fight. Joe
Jaffee was famous. The man who had bolted a Mafia family and gone straight when he was a young lad in the fifties.
And with the family millions had endowed chairs, backed
sociologists studying organized crime, founded drug treatment clinics. A real American success story.

"Are you following in your father's footsteps?"

He frowned. "I don't exactly want to walk in anybody's
footsteps. But if you're asking what I think of my father, I
think he made the right move. He and I have had arguments, but they're over strategy, not over the basics."

"Okay."

"He'll be sixty this winter. We're cutting down some on
his duties. He's moving mostly into the foundation work.
Me, I'm taking over a lot of the business administration."

"I see. You're controlling megabucks, then."

"Yup."

"I guess somebody has to do it." I drank a little more of the bug juice.

"You aren't asking me if I know who you are."

"You already know. I'm the one who got blown up."

"That was a horrible thing."

Was he sorry? Did he look guilty? Beats me. But I wouldn't have trusted him with a July Fourth firecracker right then.

We lingered over drinks. We'd arrived here at three. At about four he said, "Let's walk through the neighborhood."

"Okay."

"Are you well enough?"

"No problem."

There was a lot left of the Italian district of North Avenue, despite a lot of civic grumbling that it was not what it used to be. We stopped at a sidewalk café and drank espresso. I was feeling dizzy again, but the espresso cleared that right up. Mine is the sort of metabolism that requires periodic infusions of caffeine.

Dry leaves tumbled past, and some of them scudded up against our feet. There was a light breeze from Lake Michigan that had picked up the scents of hot dogs and automobiles on its way to us. The sun was getting low behind us, and while it was warm, it was a warm fall day, not a warm spring day. The promise was snow and ice.

I could see that he was studying the remnants of my bruises. Out of the blue, he asked: "Have you thought about retiring?"

"What! At my age?"

"You won't always be that age."

"I'm a spring chicken."

"Don't answer everything I say with a smart remark. I'm wondering seriously how your kind of career develops. Right now I suppose you run out and grab people and ask them questions."

"Some."

"And follow them up on their answers and sometimes beard strange characters in their dens, and so on."

"Sure."

"Right now you have the energy. But what about ten years from now, or twenty, when you're tired of it?"

"I plan to settle down and write a best-seller."

"See? Why won't you be serious?"

"Isn't it possible that I *am* serious?"

"Maybe."

"Anyway, I don't see what's worrying you about it."

"You were injured Saturday. You could have been killed. Have you been hurt on the job before?"

"Not exactly like that. A few sticky incidents."

"You know, the average Italian family doesn't want its daughters doing tough-guy work. Most of them would rather they didn't work at all."

"I know. My father and I don't always see eye to eye, either."

He looked at me speculatively. I had said not one word about pursuing the Sugarman murder. We had not mentioned Louise more than tangentially, just in the sense that her injury and mine had the same cause. But he spoke as if he knew I would continue to research her murder, and there was a hint that he believed it would be dangerous.

Was he warning me not to?

"How about dinner?" he asked.

LA DOLCE PESCHE WAS high Italian. And high Italian is that which there is nothing more formal than. There was a silver peach tree in the lobby, and the lobby itself was pink Italian marble.

"I look like a funeral!" I said to him, horrified at my black clothes in this place.

"No, you don't. You look beautiful."

He was bowed through the restaurant as if God had arrived. I was, too, by association. Seated at a table that resembled a pink linen wedding cake, he said, "It isn't everybody who can wear black. It's good with your dark eyes and dark hair. You look like a contessa."

Oh, well. If he's going to put it that way—

Lovely soup with tiny prawns. Bread sticks as thin as oat straws.

When Charles got up, probably to go to the men's room to get his gun from behind the toilet, I started to blow out one of the candles in the little cluster in crystal holders on the table. My intent was to ask him to relight it. Then I would find out whether his lighter was a square black box. But I realized that the hovering waiters would immediately sweep in and relight it for him.

"Don't you smoke?" I said, flat out, when he came back.

"Yes. I thought I shouldn't. Cigarette smoke can make you sick if you've had a head injury."

"No, I'm fine."

He did not take out his cigarettes then, but after the entrée, while we were puzzling over dessert, he reached for his cigarette case. It was a flat gold rectangle, thin and elegant. He started to reach for a lighter. Three waiters reached for theirs and began to converge. I was shouting, Wait! Wait! in my head. Charles's lighter came out of his breast pocket at the same instant that three hands with lighters appeared before him. His lighter was ebony.

The smallest, most active waiter made the running and had a flame in front of Charles fractionally before the other two, or Charles himself. Never mind. I had seen what Charles carried, and it was black. And square.

WE HAD LEFT MY car at my place and gone to Boney's, et cetera, in his little Lancia, so that was what Charles drove me home in. He walked me up the stairs to my second-floor door.

I said, "Good night. It was a lovely dinner." And it certainly had been.

"It's only nine."

"I'll invite you in some other time. Right now I'm coddling my head injury."

With the door closed, I listened to him walk lazily down the stairs.

Why is it I am automatically suspicious of men whose nails are carefully manicured? It's not that dirt or a blunt cut is especially attractive. Is it that such men seem too careful—read scared? Or anxious? But Charles's careful barbering, meticulous tailoring, and precise manicuring gave me different doubts from the way I felt about some such men. Charles was no peacock. More like a panther. He felt dangerous.

SIX

WHEN YOU'RE WORKING freelance, you can't allow your-self to become wrapped up in one project to the extent of developing nothing else. If you do, you will hand in a piece, feeling very proud of yourself, and then realize you're fresh out of ideas and have no "savings account" of research and notes for a new project.

Of course, I usually have a current, flat-out work pro-ject. That means begging for interviews, doing library re-search, calling informants—whatever. In addition, I'm playing with the material. A piece always needs a grabber, something to start with that makes people want to read it. It needs a tenor, a tone of its own, whether indignant or folksy or laudatory. It needs an overarching theme. And it needs a punch line. Sometimes these come to me instantly, along with the basic idea. More often they take hours or weeks of work.

Ordinarily I also have a project that is essentially fin-ished. I try to put it aside for a couple of days if I can and then reread it for smoothing before handing it in. The smoothing process is like ironing linen. It fights back, but when it's done, it's *soooo* crisp.

I always try to keep a "back-burner" project simmering, too. I have to be sure there is really a subject in it to be in-vestigated and that there is enough material to make an ar-ticle out of it. This is like panning for gold: You ask whether the stream is productive enough for you to camp there awhile.

And last are the distant possibilities. They are like the ice skates in the back left corner of the closet behind the out-grown tennis shoes. There if you need them and want to pull them out. I collect clippings, write myself notes, names, addresses, smart remarks, and salt them away in big brown accordion folders.

When a piece is actively brewing, I always try to sell it even before it's written.

BY TEN THE NEXT morning, Tuesday, I was at the *Chicago Today* office. Hal Briskman was my contact there.

"Hey, Hal, would you like a story on Louise Sugarman?"

"Babe, I know you were nearly blown up with her, but personal anguish is out this month—"

"No, that isn't—"

"It's dead. We've had too many diseases-of-the-month made-for-TV movies. Tragedy of the month. Survival story of the month. Social pathology of the month. Can't sell 'em."

"Hal—"

"And besides, it's last week's news. With our lead time, we could have civil war in Canada before you—"

"Hal!"

"What?"

"Will you let me speak! I can't imagine how you ever interviewed anybody. In your *younger days*," I said nastily.

"I didn't. I did think pieces, right from the start."

"Sure. And you have a bridge you'd like to sell."

"Good news, sweetie. Your pal Mike should be back from the assignment tonight. A day early."

"That's swell. Now may I ask the question I came in to ask?"

"Shoot. My patience is immense."

"Suppose I find out who killed Louise Sugarman?"

He was silent. With Hal this is major reaction time.

He stroked his chin and looked off into space. "Demonstrable? Provable?"

"'How I Discovered Her Killer for the Police.'"

"How are you gonna do that?"

"I was there. I remember the scene."

"What can you do the police can't do?"

"Picture it, for one thing. I was facing the whole crowd; no one else was. Except Louise."

"You saw somebody do something suspicious? Because if you did—"

"I should tell the police. I know. I'm going to tell them everything I remember. I play fair. Usually. But the feel of the different people—how they were standing, body English—all that should give me an edge. An edge the police don't have."

"And a risk the police don't share. This is dangerous."

"You've got a reporter in Beirut, Hal?"

"All right. All right."

"Deal?"

"We can't run anything libelous. No speculation about a perp in advance of an indictment."

"I'll give you facts. Or better yet, the inside story the moment of the arrest."

"Big talk."

"You only pay for the product. Deal?"

More silence. Then he named a figure I had never heard out of his mouth before. I mean, what he pays for a feature can usually keep me going for a whole week and a half. Now we were talking six months and maybe even a little left over for a few days in Key West.

"I'll be back when I've got it," I said.

Big talk, indeed. But I had to pin him down. You need to be able to go in later and say, "You told me you wanted it!"

In fact, I wasn't all that interested in the money. Oh, I was interested in the *money,* in the sense that I wouldn't give it back. I am always financially on the edge. Currently the gas gauge on my Bronco didn't work because the float had broken off, and I couldn't afford to fix it, so I had to keep guessing how much gas I had. But I would have pursued the Louise Sugarman case, anyway. The first day after the killing, I thought I was furious. It was true enough. But the more I found out about Louise, the angrier I got. People liked her. People missed her.

This was going to be a personal quest.

OF COURSE, ONE OF the problems was precisely that people liked Louise. People around her, that is. It was getting to be harder and harder to picture them as guilty.

Chances were, Louise's thin, scholarly husband had not blown her up. Chances were her co-workers hadn't, either. While the theory is that the nearest and dearest should be suspected first in any murder—and that theory isn't any too shabby, either—it didn't seem right in this case. I had started to have serious doubts, even before I remembered Charles Jaffee's hasty exit from the reception hall.

What this meant was, I had better look into Louise Sugarman as a public person.

It was altogether too simple, though, just to say that somebody hated her for her stand on drugs. Not *false*. Hate her, they surely did, and in their thousands. But by itself not an entirely convincing motive for murder. I can summarize in one word what I find convincing as a motive for murder: money.

Find a person who had a financial reason to fear Louise Sugarman's public position and you've really got something. The economics of a political stand like hers was not my field. In fact, economics has always seemed to me mystifying in its jargon and too late in its explanations of what's going to happen. People who teach it don't seem to be able to use it to make money on the stock market. However, rule 8c in reporting is go to the source.

The economist on the ill-fated panel was Robert Q. Erdmann. He was a professor at Lehigh College in Chicago. I could kill two birds with one stone: find out about the economics of the repeal movement and at the same time see what I thought of Erdmann himself. Efficiency is my middle name. I call it efficiency when I want to praise it. Other times you can call it laziness.

A phone call set up an appointment for that afternoon.

"OH, MY DEAR GIRL!" Professor Erdmann said.

He must have seen me bristle, because he immediately added: "All right, all right. I know you're not a child. But you talk like a child."

"Professor Erdmann, you said that a person who sells drugs doesn't feel morally blameworthy because if he doesn't do it somebody else will. All I said was, that doesn't absolve him. Because if everybody refused to sell drugs, there wouldn't *be* any pushers." Of the two people I had pegged as professors at the reception, Erdmann was not the one who chewed on things. He now demonstrated that he was an eyebrow raiser.

"*Of course,* if everybody stopped, it wouldn't happen. But that's ridiculous. It's weak thinking. It begs the question, because it's not the way things really *are.* If everybody in Israel and the Arab states all just stopped retaliating for past atrocities, they could negotiate a peace. If the Catholics and Protestants in Northern Ireland would just stop fighting and talk, they would all benefit. If everybody in the U.S. just sent in a dollar, we could get the homeless off the streets. If people would wait until they were married to have sex, there would be less venereal disease. If everybody—"

"All right. All right. I see what you mean."

I was writing, but he didn't ask if I could keep up. He went on, speaking fast.

"But look at it. The problem is that this never happens. Never does everybody all get together on anything. It's the same with the question of the drug trade. It won't happen. The problem is just too large.

"Morally speaking, if I go out on the street and mug somebody, that person very, very, very most likely would not have been mugged if not for me. But if I go down to the corner of Addison and Kedzie and pick up several ounces of cocaine from a wholesaler and take it to the corner of

Monroe and Wabash and give it to ten retailers, nothing will have happened that wouldn't have happened, anyway. If I *destroy it,* it won't make any difference, either. The slush pile of drugs is so huge and the ways to fill in are so many that my action won't make any difference at all. If the supply of some drugs dries up temporarily in an area, it's easy enough just to turn out a few extra ounces of designer drugs in somebody's basement.

"The problem is economic. The drug laws have created a pusher class. Created. You could do it with anything. When you outlaw something, you make the price go up. You make it valuable and worth pushing. It was done with alcohol during Prohibition. We created organized crime. And during Prohibition, contrary to what most people believe, the consumption of alcohol *increased.*

"Take—take anything people really want and some people really need. Take coffee, for instance. The ancient Egyptians, in fact, actually did outlaw coffee."

"I didn't know that."

"Well, in the history of man, almost anything people enjoy has been made illegal at some time or other. Now, say you make coffee illegal. Possession is a misdemeanor. Sale is a felony. Do people stop drinking coffee?"

"Well, actually, I might mug somebody for a cup of coffee."

"There are theories that there are thirty million borderline depressives in this country who self-medicate with caffeine. And do pretty well with it. There are certainly over a hundred million people who drink coffee every day. You outlaw it, they'll buy it underground. Then what will happen, Ms. Marsala?"

"Uh—the price will go up."

"Right. The price will go up. Then a purer form, pure caffeine, will come on the market, because it's easier to transport secretly and easier to hide. But the purer form is also more dangerous. You can die from an overdose. Scare stories come out in the papers of people dying from overdoses. That's horrible. People are terrified, so we raise the criminal penalties even higher for selling pure caffeine. That makes it really risky to transport, so the price *really* shoots up. Thousands of dollars an ounce. White gold. Distributors for the mob are killed for skimming tiny amounts. Murders! The foul smell of organized crime! Sleazy runners, fast boats from coffee-growing countries, drug wars!

"Previously law abiding people are drawn in because there is so *much* money, and besides, they don't feel it's wrong. People will get their caffeine somehow. The stench of crime and death hangs over the whole operation, so Congress cracks down. Much harsher penalties. What happens then? Come on, Ms. Marsala, tell me. What happens then?"

"The price goes up farther."

"Righto! The price goes up farther. The supply can only be kept going by big, *big, BIG* crime organizations. People with the money to bribe customs officials. People who can bribe the police. The scarcity *produces the money to overcome itself.* Major Mafia boys come in, types who can afford oceangoing boats with several thousand horsepower. The price gets so high that they can afford to fly in batches of caffeine by air and then abandon the planes. Then what happens, Ms. Marsala?"

"Um—"

"I'll tell you what happens. Substitutes. People start distilling chocolate for its theobromine. People pretend to have asthma to get theophylline. Doctors are corrupted. Hobbyists invent chemical substitutes in their basements. Then the substitutes have to be outlawed in turn."

Finally, he ran down and stopped. I asked: "But how realistic is this, really? Would people really purify the—the active component in coffee when coffee was perfectly good by itself?"

"It's *exactly* what happened with opium."

"Explain."

"People had been smoking opium for centuries. Possibly millennia. It wasn't all that harmful a habit, as things go. Might get reddish eyes. Dream a little. But it wasn't very strong. It wasn't very pure—just the dried sap."

"But you hear about opium dens—"

"Sure you do. To Europeans in the 1800s they were exotic and scary. But they were a hell of a lot quieter than any bar after a Chicago Bears game. It didn't lead to fights in the streets. And the people could get up and go to work the next day."

"Really?"

"Really. Then there were the opium scares, then the need to transport the stuff in a compact form. People already knew you could concentrate it; the concentrated form was used as an anesthetic. Morphine. As the laws got tougher, heroin was derived from morphine."

"Do you—I have to ask—"

"What? Sell drugs? If I sold drugs for a profit, the last thing I'd want is for them to be legalized."

"But as a user you might."

"Possibly I might."

"Sorry."

"People always think you have an ax to grind, don't they? No, I don't use drugs. Actually, I couldn't do drugs and still write about this safely. I don't drink, either. Or smoke. Matter of fact, I'm a vegetarian, too. My interest stems strictly from economic analysis. And maybe indignation. I hate to see large numbers of people behaving stupidly."

"Specify, please."

"I don't like the fact that we're causing people to cause other people to try drugs."

"Supply and demand?"

"Well, sure. There are enormous financial incentives to people to go out and *convert* another bunch of people to drugs. Especially if the first group needs money to support their own habits."

"Give me a quote," I said, writing.

"If there wasn't any money in it, people wouldn't be pushers."

WELL, I DIDN'T KNOW that I agreed with the fellow. Personally, I still thought legalization was dangerous. I had my own reason to loathe drugs. My youngest brother, Teddy, had more or less burned out his brain on acid and PCP. But that wasn't the point at this instant. I could add two and two.

What happened when the war on drugs heated up? What happened when the borders were tightened? The marginal operators were driven out. People faint of heart or without connections.

And the well connected took over.

Who is the granddaddy of all connections? Who is the Big Connection?

The mob.

Who has the money to buy boats and airplanes? The connections to bribe customs officials? The network to make the stuff vanish into its pipelines as soon as it hits shore?

The mob.

Who has the most to lose if drugs are decriminalized?

The mob.

Who could easily find the materials for a bomb to blow up Louise Sugarman?

The mob. Hell, they probably had a specialized subcontractor who did only minibombs for close-up work.

This seemed to me an excellent time to go to Captain McCoo.

"I HAVE A CAPTAIN'S meeting in half an hour."

"No, you don't, McCoo. That's like the check's in the mail or I can't come because my grandmother just died."

"Well, listen to you! You have this sherry-induced flash of memory when? Night before last. You were going to let me know as soon as you remembered, right? Now all of a sudden you're in a big hurry to talk with me."

"Oh, stop pretending to fuss. You're just worried I'll get into trouble."

"How are you, by the way?"

"Perfectly all right."

"Have any headaches?"

I contemplated lying, but with him I couldn't. "Some."

He sat down, poured two cups of coffee, and added cream to mine because he knew I liked it. McCoo's office is big but Spartan. It is all bookcases and files, floor to ceiling and wall to wall. He says he doesn't like to yell for help when he needs to look something up. There isn't even a rug. He likes to sit in his wheeled desk chair and scoot over to a file or bookcase. His only nonaustere item is an expensive drip coffee maker, a grinder, and a supply of Kenyan beans. He says they are actually raised in Uganda but packaged in Kenya.

"McCoo, what would you do if you couldn't get coffee?"

"Oh, fall down and scream. Go nuts. Kill. Why?"

"Just curious."

"All right. Shoot. You had a flash, and now you see the crowd in the fatal reception room. It's engraved on your mind."

"Charlie Jaffee was there. You know the Jaffees?"

"Yes, Cat." Oozing patience, was McCoo.

"The bomb goes off. I'm hurtling from my chair, I suppose, though it didn't feel like that. I'm turned by the force of it, I guess, and there is Charles Jaffee. He turned toward the exit door, with a small, square black box in his hand. Then I'm on the floor. He slips the box in his pocket, and he's gone."

"And you think the box means something?"

"Maybe. When I first caught a glimpse of him, he had it sort of aimed at us."

"How do you aim a square thing?"

"All I mean is he had his arm slightly extended and the box held—um—so that I could see the end of it. You know what I mean; his fingers weren't around it like they usually are when you just hold an object. Like this!" I aimed the top of the empty coffee cup toward McCoo.

"Maybe it's his cigarette case. Or lighter."

"Well . . . it could be."

"You checked."

"Sure."

"Oh, Cat! What if it *had* been a—you should pardon the expression—clue. Who's going to back you up when you're out there alone?"

"Me. I don't need backup."

"Don't try so hard. Sometimes you have to be scared—"

"I'm not scared of Charlie Jaffee."

"Maybe you should be. He's a charity big boy, and he's legit, I guess. But who ever knows? Even if he's okay, what happens if you get near the real killer?"

"Well, I'm cautious—"

"You can't be cautious twenty-four hours a day. Suppose somebody bides his time?"

"I'll see him first."

"Louise Sugarman didn't get a chance."

"Oh, horsepukky."

"If that doesn't scare you, what does?"

"Come on, McCoo."

"No. I think you can't admit you're scared of anything. I think you have a problem."

"Sure. Some things scare me."

"Name one."

"Um—water."

"Water? *Water?*"

"Yeah."

"Why?"

"I can't swim."

"You can't swim?"

"Stop repeating everything I say."

"Everybody can swim. I can swim. I grew up in an inner-city school. I mean, it was so inner city, it was landlocked. No pool. And I can swim."

"McCoo, you could float." He wasn't actually fat, but he was squarely built.

"Why can't you?"

I stood up. Then I sat down. McCoo stared at me. He knew he'd hit a nerve. "I can't swim because my father had the idea that you make kids learn to swim by throwing them in the water. So he did. At Foster Beach. When I was seven. I almost drowned. The lifeguard pulled me out and yelled at my father, and then he punched the lifeguard, and I never went back in the water again if I could possibly help it."

McCoo simply let that fade into the distance. He gave it maybe a minute and a half, which is a long time if you're sitting staring at each other. But I wasn't going to talk first. Finally, he said, "About Jaffee. I don't let cops go into that kind of situation alone. Not that this was that kind of situation."

"Why not? You think the Jaffees are angels? What if that philanthropic business is just a cover? What if the mob assigned one family like that to *appear* to bolt the Mafia just so they could infiltrate the establishment?"

"Not impossible. But unlikely."

"And who do you think is making the most money from drugs in this country?"

"The mob."

"So who do you think is most threatened by a legalization move?"

"The mob."

"Well, then?"

"Cat, what exactly do you think the black box was?"

"A remote detonator."

"And what door was Charlie Jaffee slipping out of?"

"The exit, the fire exit on my left. The one with the red exit sign over it. I can *see* it."

"And that was immediately after the blast?"

"Within a second. I was still falling."

"Sorry, Cat. Try again."

"Why?"

"We found the detonator apparatus. In the room."

I was stunned. Then I said, "Near the door? He dropped it after I blacked out?"

"On the other side of the room, Cat. To your far right. Near the windows."

SEVEN

"IT CAN'T BE," I said.

"Oh, come on. So you have to revise your theory."

"Well, then, what was the black box?"

"A tape recorder? Maybe he's going to record his talk, or everybody's talks. More likely a cigarette lighter. Actually, he told one of the policemen outdoors that he had been inside."

"So—then why did he leave?"

"Cat, if I had a dollar for every person who left the scene of a crime simply because he didn't want to be tied up there for hours—"

"You'd what?"

"I could retire." He grinned.

"Would you if you could?"

"Okay, you got me back," he said seriously. "No. If I won the lottery tomorrow, I'd be back here the next day. Now let's leave the soul-searching and you tell me a few things. I would like to know whether the bomb was planted before or after Louise sat down. Either somebody guessed she'd sit there, or the bomb was meant for anybody and everybody, or after you two sat, the killer came over and dropped the—I don't want to put it in your mind what it was—um, thing there."

"You want me to cast my mind back, go into a trance, and picture the whole scene."

"Yup."

"Trade me?"

"What for what?"

"My memory for your list of everybody who was there. And whether you can eliminate any of them."

"As a good citizen, Cat, your duty is to assist the police."

"I work better when I'm inspired."

"Off the record?"

"I'll tell you what. I will clear with you first *anything* I write on the murder before I submit it."

"You really want this."

"I *deserve* it."

"I agree."

"We're going to the sofa and sitting down. Nobody follows us. Nobody approaches us after we sit. We're talking. She is sitting on my right."

"Now look to your far right, past Louise Sugarman. What do you see?"

"Well, next to her is a table."

"That's what I want. Describe it."

"Well, it's that Formica stuff, or whatever, that institutions use. Grained to look like wood. Her purse is on it. It's a—sort of beige cloth purse. The purse is to the back. Nearer the front is an ashtray. Near—not in—the ashtray is an empty cigarette pack."

"It was there before you sat down?"

"It must have been."

"Why do you think it's empty?"

"Uh—I don't know. It's been opened and then left there. I guess I assumed it was empty because it had been abandoned."

"How do you know it's been opened?"

"The cellophane is off it. The tax stamp is torn open, and part of the foil is hanging loose."

"What brand is it?"

I couldn't see it. Yes, I could. "Um—it's half red and half white. Wait. Carlton 120's."

"That's right. Now tell me about the ashtray."

"Tin. The cheap kind they use so nobody wants to steal them. There's a cigarette in it."

"Stubbed out?"

"Yes."

"How?"

"How was it stubbed out?"

"Yes."

"Like somebody had pushed down on it and then bent it over."

"Like a kind of flattened letter *J?*"

"Yes."

"Anything else on the table?"

"No."

"Okay, you can come out of that semitrance."

"What did you mean when you said that was right?"

"The explosive was in a Carlton 120's package. We found pieces of it with chemical blown into the inner sides of the paper."

Then, at McCoo's request, I painted the picture I had memorized when I was at John's house of the people near us when the bomb blew. Dr. Lloyd (I thought it was he) munching on a roll of paper in a chair near the windows. Uncle Ben talking to a woman in lavender, her back to us. Erdmann gesturing with a pen. Torkel Gates near the munchies table, fiddling with something. Lt. Stan Gotchka facing us. Leota Parks as a less focused pink blob. The student waiter and waitress. A man I didn't know off to the left.

"And this group blocked your view of the people behind them?"

"Sure. It wasn't that big a room."

"Anything else?"

"You know, this isn't like taking a photo. You don't get everything clear, and if you think too much, you may make up things."

"Okay. I must say, Cat, your memory squares with what everybody else has told us. You're not bad."

"Thanks. Reward me. Tell me who exactly was there."

There were, including me and Charles Jaffee, and excluding Louise Sugarman, twenty people in that reception room. McCoo's list looked like this:

City of Chicago alderman Juan Garcia
Dr. Cameron Lloyd
Betty Lloyd
Clarella Jones, student, hired to pass munchies
Norbert E. Lillie, student, hired to pass sherry
Michelle Zuger, student, hired to pass sherry
Morton C. Levy, administration, University of Chicago
Sally Levy
Barbara Parson, professor, University of Chicago
Bing Parson III
Alan C. Allen, Immigration and Naturalization Service
Professor Robert Q. Erdmann
Catherine Marsala
Charles Jaffee, CC Charities
Leota Parks, northern Illinois PTA
Glen Barton, DEA
Ben Hoskinson, PASA
Torkel Gates, his assistant
Max Sugarman
Lt. Stan Gotchka, Chicago Police Department

"Twenty," I said. "Who can we exclude?"

"Anybody who had both hands busy with anything demonstrably legitimate."

"The female student with food and the male student with the sherry, then. I saw them clearly. Both had both hands on their trays when the bomb blew."

"So did the one who was out of your sight."

"Okay. We cross off Jones, Lillie, and Zuger."

"Cross out anybody who had his or her back to you."

"Why?"

"They had to see to point the remote detonator."

"The woman in lavender. I don't know her name."

"Professor Barbara Parson."

"You even know their clothing? When you people do interviews, you do a good job."

"Shucks. It's nuthin'."

"So can we eliminate the people out of my sight?"

"I already have crossed off everybody who was too far away or in back of too many other people—"

"Not on just their say-so?"

"What do you take me for? No, these are verified by at least one unrelated person nearby. You'd be surprised how well people remember where they were when a bomb goes off. And who they were near. They're not as good at what they were doing before and after."

"Come on, then. Who?"

"Alan C. Allen of the INS, the administrator Morton Levy, Bing Parson and Sally Levy, who were *very,* very close in the corner—"

"Don't get sidetracked here."

"Betty Lloyd and Juan Garcia—"

"Who were very, very close?"

"Who were very loudly arguing."

"Leaving us—"

"Leaving me, thanks to your assistance, only seven real suspects: Dr. Lloyd, Max Sugarman, Ben Hoskinson (sorry about that, Cat), Torkel Gates, Glen Barton, Leota Parks, and Professor Erdmann."

"Eight."

"What?"

"Stan Gotchka."

"He's a Chicago *policeman!*"

I didn't say anything, but looked him steadily in his big brown eyes.

"Eight," he said. "To be thorough."

"And the man I didn't recognize must be this Glen Barton from the DEA."

"Looks like it."

"Okay. If I've been some help, then good. You said anybody with his back to me couldn't have done it. Because of the sort of detonator. I'd like to know more about it. Tit for tat, you should pardon the expression. Let me talk with your explosives expert."

"I was just about to do that." He mashed down on his desk button with a large, flat thumb.

"SO THESE TWO LITTLE triple-A batteries could go end to end?"

"Oh, sure. End to end as long as it's positive to negative. Like a flashlight. No problem. Or side by side. It doesn't matter as long as you make a complete circuit."

"If they were end to end, what would hold them in place?"

"Well, anything would be okay. A tube of cardboard. Metal. I suppose you could even hold them in your bare hand, but it would be sort of awkward. You'd need the wire to touch the bottom of one and run up through this on-off button and through the infrared device and then to the top of the second battery. Complete the circuit. Simple. It's not big, you know. About as big as a cigarette. The actual detonator is in the bomb package. Strictly speaking, this is only the signal device. Basically a specialized flashlight."

We were chatting in the Bomb and Arson Department. Krumpp was a man with very short legs, very long arms, and very large hands. But deft. He switched the batteries around and moved wires as if he were choreographing them. I could imagine him defusing a bomb. He was also terribly cheery.

"Infrared?" I repeated.

"Yeah, sure. Like in your television channel changer."

"That can't be right."

"Why not?" His tone was patient but indulgent.

"My channel-changing remote thing can't be infrared. Because I have a friend, and he has a Siberian husky who has a chain collar, and when he comes over and his collar clinks—the husky, I mean—he changes the channels. And he certainly isn't infrared."

"You must have an *old* set," he said happily.

"Um, yes. It's pretty old."

"Because they haven't been manufactured that way in ages. That was ultrasonic. It's all infrared pulses now. And you can see why, if you're making a bomb, you wouldn't want to use an ultrasonic device. I mean, there you are, walking around with the thing in your pocket, and somebody's dog sets it off?"

"I can see that."

"Or any stray noise."

"Right. So let me get this straight. If the thing that sets it off uses infrared light, I suppose there has to be a straight line between the source of the infrared and the bomb. If somebody stepped in the way, it would be like casting a shadow, so to speak."

"Yes, you'd need to aim at the explosive. Or at the receiver attached to the detonator attached to the explosive, strictly speaking."

"Which is why a person standing behind a bunch of other people couldn't have done it."

"Sure."

"Would you have to aim carefully?"

"Naw. Not too much. The beam would go out in a cone shape, like a flashing beam. Simple."

"And the explosive? You could get that and the receiver and the detonator that makes the explosives explode—all that inside a cigarette package?"

"No problem. Although—"

"What?"

"I think they made it easy for themselves by using the long-size cigarettes."

"Now, would they have to leave an opening so the 'eye' in the bomb could see the infrared?"

"Oh, sure. But no problem. No problem. Just a little peephole would do it."

"Could they direct the explosion? I mean like aim it?"

"Sure! You hollow the explosive. Make it kind of cup shaped. Put the detonator in the cup part and the force will mainly all go out that way. You have to think of explosive as not something that goes bang instantly. So you start the combustion on the inside of the cup shape and the exploding gases will all blast out that way. Easiest thing in the world.''

"So what exactly was found on the windowsill?"

"The batteries, the wires, the infrared light, and the switch."

"And no hint what it had been inside of?"

"Nope."

"And no fingerprints?"

"Nope."

"No fingerprints on the cigarette package, either?"

"Nope. The paper was somewhat charred, though."

"Well, thank you, Mr. Krumpp."

"No problem."

So CHARLES JAFFEE WAS out of the running for murderer. No way he could have used the infrared device while he was going out of the room by a door on my far left and then have thrown that stuff—the batteries, wire, light, and switch button—over to the windowsill on my far right. It wouldn't have stayed intact—somebody would have noticed—and it probably wouldn't have landed on the windowsill, either.

What was more, even if he had a second infrared device—and why should he?—when he was going out the exit on our left, my body and Louise's, as we sat on the sofa, "shadowed" the cigarette package on our right from any beam he could have aimed its way. Plus he owned a black cigarette lighter.

Which meant I had gone out to a fancy restaurant with a well-dressed, handsome man who was philanthropic and also extremely rich and spent the whole evening suspecting him of a murder he had not committed.

Drat.

Between wasting time suspecting the wrong person and probably permanently repulsing Charles Jaffee, my bad luck for the day must be over. Mike was due back tonight, and I intended to go out and relax. Have some fun. I'd earned it. Nothing else could go wrong.

MIKE BREEZED IN. Like a wind off the prairies, bringing rumors of a hundred wild flowers. He had been researching a piece on riverboat captains, some of whom, aged but loquacious, still lived in the towns along the upper Mississippi. One of these captains lived on a drydocked riverboat that functioned as a summertime restaurant. Mike had a hundred stories.

"But the best story is," he said as he was sweeping me out the door, "there's a tour agency that's actually rebuilding three of the old boats. A stern-wheeler and two side-wheelers. The hulls are going to be completely new, so they'll float."

"Well, that sounds like they have their priorities straight."

"But they're keeping all the superstructure. All the old woodwork. They're going to ply the big river again."

We ran down the stoop and over to his car. I forgot to ask where we were going in such a hurry.

"So they've hired my two favorite old captains on as—"

"Not as captains, surely?"

"At ninety-two and ninety-six? No. As consultants, though. Paid. Which is, as somebody I knew used to say, not the onliest of it. They want them to ride along on the trips and tell stories. And since they've spent pretty much the last fifty or sixty years telling those stories over and over to people who were tired of listening to them, this gives them a whole new lease on life. In the spring, when the first boat is ready, you and I can go on it, down to New Orleans."

We pulled into a parking lot next to a downtown revival movie theater. It was showing *Key Largo*. One of my ten top favorites.

"The early show," Mike said. "Then we eat."

An hour and half later, Lauren Bacall opened the hurricane shutters on a new, bright day. Some of the audience laughed, as some always do. The gesture was symbolic, of course, and probably seemed more subtle when it was filmed than it does now. I wondered whether any of the people who laughed realize how symbolic movies are now or how obvious they're going to seem in thirty years, when the symbols have been overused.

"Pizza," Mike said.

"Mama Z's?"

"Let's."

"It's two blocks," I said. "Let's walk."

He swung my hand as we went. "I've got a new project."

"Yum. What?"

"Judges. Why does somebody want to be a judge?"

"Power?"

"Maybe. But it's pretty limited power. Anyway, I won't find out until I interview some. And their friends."

"Will they let you interview them?"

"The judges? Won't know until I try. But it'll be great!"

I was beginning to feel uneasy. Mike is always hyper. His enthusiasm is part of why he's fun. But still— "Do you think you'll ever halfway settle down?"

"Cat, I've had the same job for four years. I've lived in the same building for three."

"But the job consists of running from place to place and from one project to another. And you're away from your apartment more than you're there. I mean, you have such a huge need for novelty—"

"And so little tolerance for repetition. I know that. But I channel it, don't I?"

Mama Z's was crowded, but there was a table for two. The earliest dinner crowd must have been there while we were at the movie.

"Anchovies?" Mike said.

"Rather have sausage. And hot peppers."

"Giant pizza," he told the waitress, "with sausage, hot peppers, extra cheese, and two beers."

My heart sank. "Why don't we have Coke?"

"No, no. Two beers."

I let the waitress get out of earshot. "I knew it!" I said. "I should have known it, anyway."

"Cat, one beer never hurt anybody."

"It does when one beer's not the end of it."

"I am perfectly all right."

"You've been drinking on your trip."

"One beer with dinner. I stuck to it perfectly. Cat, don't ruin the evening."

Ruined was the word for it. I felt as if I were standing on the side of a mountain just before the avalanche and knew it was going to happen and couldn't do a thing to stop it. Leaving him wouldn't help. Calling a friend wouldn't help. Anything short of tying his hands and feet together wouldn't help. Probably my best bet was to stick around and try to distract him.

TRY TO DISTRACT THE tide coming in. Halfway through the pizza he ordered another beer. By then I refused and went over to Pepsi. I'd soon need a clear head.

As we left Mama's I tried to talk cheerfully. He had drunk three beers altogether.

"Let's go to my place," I said.

"Okay. But let's stop in Giorgio's first and see the news."

"I've got a TV, too."

"Won't take a minute. It's on the way to the car."

It took an hour and two bourbons. A 7-Up for me. He knew what I was doing but didn't remark. Neither did I. Believe me, arguing with a person in his state makes it worse.

I got him to leave. He found another bar across the street from the car. Another bourbon. We got back out before the second. He fumbled for his keys. I said, "I'll drive."

He turned them over quickly. This is one of the reasons you're better off not starting a fight.

"We could go to Lou's," he said, naming his favorite bar.

"My place."

"You're pissed, aren't you?"

"Disappointed, maybe."

"Well, you can let me out right here."

I wanted to. But that way lay a bar-to-bar-to-bar evening with no one to protect him, a possible mugging, a possible arrest.

"I can't let you out; it's your car."

"You have sompin' to drink at your place?"

"Oh, sure," I said. There wasn't much. Two beers, maybe some brandy. The less the better. He might fall asleep before he found out how little there was.

"Oooo-kay."

BUT HE FOUND THE brandy first, on the same shelf above my sink where the spices and tomato sauce lived. Sauce for the goose and sauce for the gander. To my dismay, the bottle was half full. I grabbed at it, thinking to pour some of it out, but he saw what I was going to do.

"No!" he said, clutching it to his bosom.

Long John Silver shook his feathers. *"Braaak!"* he shouted. Mike didn't hear him.

Long John said, *"Awk!* Wee sleekit, cow'rin, tim'rous beastie! *Braaak!"* I couldn't agree more. But I ignored him.

"Here," I said to Mike. "How about potato chips?"

But he was on his way to the sofa, tacking against a non-existent wind. He flopped heavily, stuck out his feet.

"Here are the potato chips, Mike."

"Put 'em right there."

He patted the sofa next to him, I put them down. He ignored them. I opened the bag. He took a swallow from the bottle, tipping it up. I handed him the bag. He pushed it away.

"Well!" I said brightly. "Let's get the late news."

"Mmm-hm." He agreed, drinking. It was scary how fast the brandy level was going down. I turned on the TV and turned it up loud. Then I left the room. He didn't notice.

I telephoned from my bedroom, where he wouldn't hear me.

Mike's AA sponsor and friend is a man we call Yosemite Sam. His real name is Sam Yusimele, which I think is Syrian. Unless it's Turkish or possibly southern Bulgarian.

"Sam! This is Cat. Thank God you're home."

"Mike, I suppose." Sam sighed.

"He must have started drinking yesterday or the day before."

"Didn't you notice?"

"I was in the hospital. Then he was out of town on assignment. This is the first time I've seen him in the evening in four days."

"Your place?"

"Yes."

"That was smart. Don't fight with him. I'll be there as soon as I can."

"Thanks, Sam."

"They did it for me."

I went back to the living room. There can't have been a quarter of the bottle left. Sam was half an hour away, in Oak Park. Gritting my teeth, I sat down to watch the late news. "Have a potato chip?"

"Inna minute."

Slowly, and by no means slowly enough, the level of brandy fell. My heart sank with it. Then it was gone. Some movie or other had come on TV. Mike tipped the bottle upside down, and nothing came out. He giggled.

I took the bottle and put it on the table. Half a bottle of brandy in an hour!

He mumbled something. I couldn't understand it, but instinct told me he had said, "Now where's that beer?"

"You don't want beer," I said.

"Onndt!" He shoved against me. I half stood up to get out of the way and fell sideways against the table.

"Hell!" I wasn't really hurt, but the jarring had caused my head to scream. That concussion was only 70 percent gone.

"I'll get the beer."

Out in the kitchen, I sat down, hoping he'd forget or fall asleep. While I was hoping, the doorbell rang. I'm on the third floor, but the street door downstairs doesn't lock.

I opened the door without asking who it was. In the city? Stupid!

"Never open your door without asking who it is!" Yosemite Sam said.

"I just told myself that."

Yosemite has a huge belly—beer had been his thing, in quarts—and a huge white beard. But he's only about forty-five years old. I love old Sam.

"Show me the patient."

"Follow your nose."

"To the brandy? I see what you mean."

"What now?"

"It'd be best if he went to sleep."

"Sure, but he wants beer."

"And if you don't get it for him?"

"By past experience, Sam, he's capable of going out for it. And walking in front of cars. And—jeez!"

Mike lurched to his feet. "Said you'd g'me beer!"

He ran sideways to the window, then in a half circle toward the kitchen door, in a kind of bucking Groucho Marx lope. He veered to the front door. Yosemite Sam caught him.

"Whoa, boy! Let's think this over." He whispered to me, "Get some beer and dilute it with water!"

I had just turned to go to the kitchen when Mike pushed Sam. The recoil of his own push, combined with a total lack of balance, sent him crashing into the wall behind him. For a couple of seconds he stopped breathing. His face got purplish-blue. Then he threw up. Right then the phone rang. I let it ring.

"To the bathroom!" Sam bellowed. He and I pushed Mike. Mike started to crumple. We each got an arm.

"No, not there!" Sam said as I headed Mike to the toilet. "Into the tub!"

Mike went on being sick. The place reeked of brandy. And worse. I couldn't have lifted him; I was tired already. But Sam picked Mike up as if he were a toddler and slung him into the tub, where he went on being sick.

"Cold water?" I asked. "Do we sober him up?"

"He won't sober up. He's taken in too much. Turn on medium warm."

"Okay." I felt it until it was right.

"Now we'll undress him. Rinse off the clothes as we go."

Wet clothes are almost impossible to get off a body that is determined not to help. Mike by now was semiconscious, but 100 percent complaining. With Sam holding the limp body and me pulling from the pants cuffs and sleeve cuffs, we got him undressed. The phone rang again during this process, but I couldn't leave. I sloshed out the clothes, wrung them, and put them aside, while Sam kept Mike from drowning. Then we let out the filthy water and refilled the tub with medium hot.

"We'll get him nice and relaxed and put him to bed."

After twenty minutes or so, Mike was asleep in the water. Sam hauled him out and held him upright while I dried him. We wrapped him in an old terry-cloth robe of mine, the one I usually wear. Sam carried him like a baby to the sofa, laid him down, and covered him with a blanket.

"Guaranteed for twelve hours."

"Good."

"You should change, too," he said, looking at my clothes. "He got you in a couple of places."

"Let me start the coffee first."

"I'll start the coffee and clean the rug. You change."

When I came back to the kitchen, wearing my best robe, the coffee was ready. "You want some, or will it keep you up?" I asked Sam.

"It won't keep me up, but it just might get me home."

I poured.

"Do you have any booze around here for him to get into if he wakes up? Which, mind you, I don't think he will."

"Two bottles of beer is all there is."

"Would you be upset if we poured it out?"

"I'd be delighted."

We got the beer out of the refrigerator. "Let me do it," Sam said. He uncapped both, took one in each hand, and poured both of them out at once. He held his head over the sink as he did, inhaling. "Ah!" he said in great sensual satisfaction.

"What are you doing?"

"I don't drink it, but I still love it!"

Sam poured the last drops in the palm of his hand. Then he patted them on his earlobes, the way you might with perfume. "Three years," he said. It was obvious what he meant.

Then we drank our coffee.

"Tomorrow," said Sam, "Mike will be feeling sore and sorry. I'll get here about eleven in the morning. The Rush Street AA has a noon meeting."

"Okay."

"Cheer up."

"Is it ever going to end?"

"I think so. It's a disease. Treat it, don't fight it. Let *him* fight it. You going to stand by him?"

"You know, Sam, we don't have any commitments."

"But I mean, you're not going to turn away from him?"

"I wouldn't do that."

"Sure. But I mean, you're not going to get attached to the stockbroker, are you?"

"John?"

"Yeah, John."

"No. When Mike's— When he's okay, he's more fun than anybody. More alive."

"That coffee going to keep *you* up?"

"Never. I've had such a day! Look at the clock! It's one A.M. At least nothing *else* can go wrong."

"I'll leave, then."

"Sam, thank you."

He saluted his way out the door. I picked up the coffee cups and was halfway to the kitchen when the doorbell rang. "What did you forget—?" I said, opening the door.

It was John.

"I called twice, and you didn't answer. I was worried," he said. Then he saw beyond me to Mike, asleep on the sofa, and me in my silk robe with two coffee cups.

"Oh."

I was going to say, "It's not what you think," but it could have been what he thought if things hadn't gone the way they did.

"Well, good night," he said politely, and he left.

Oh, hell.

Oh, hell, hell, hell, hell, hell, hell, hell.

EIGHT

IN GRADE SCHOOL I had teachers exactly like Leota Parks. Especially in the fourth grade, when I had Mrs. Lamb. The kind that keep lumpy ashtrays labeled Teacher on their desks. Mints in the top drawer and the whole desk smells minty. Eyeglasses on a ribbon. Ms. Parks was browner skinned than my Mrs. Lamb, but they were from the same mold. Ms. Parks was a fourth-grade teacher herself, but she was now on half duty because of her commitments to the northern Illinois PTA.

Because she had been so vitriolic when she spoke to Louise Sugarman at the reception, I had been expecting a nasty person. She wasn't. There was a little spray of lavender asters on her desk in a vase shaped like Bambi. She wore a pink sweater with a pink cardigan over it and a gray skirt. She was a brown skinned, unwrinkled woman who was probably fifty-five and looked like forty-five. She smiled and pulled up a chair for me.

Mind you, sweet or not, today, Wednesday, was Find People Who Hated Louise Sugarman Day. McCoo had challenged me to change my Charles Jaffee theory. Okay, I'm flexible.

In the field of hate candidates, Leota Parks was first on my list.

"I mentioned on the phone that I was doing an article on Louise Sugarman."

"If it's some sort of eulogy, you've come to the wrong person." She smiled and shook her head regretfully, to take the sting out of it. But she meant it just the same.

"Why is that?"

"Look, honey, how much are you gonna quote me?"

"If you want something off the record, say so. I'll respect it. I'm mostly looking for background, anyway. How people reacted to her."

"Put it this way. This—what I'm going to say is off the record, but it'll let you know where I stand. Then I'll make other comments if you want them."

"Okay."

"I detested her. Sorry to have to say it. The reason I detested Louise is simple. I thought she traded on her nice-little-lady appearance. She could get away with saying almost anything no matter how—how pernicious!—because she always looked as if she meant well. Couldn't hurt a flea. You know what I mean?"

"Yes. She certainly looked like everybody's favorite grandmother."

"You bet. Baking cookies with one hand and passing out dope with the other."

"You're not suggesting—"

"That she was a pusher? No, no, honey. Absolutely not. Just in theory. She would have had that junk available at the neighborhood store."

"Some people think it's the scarcity—"

"That makes it attractive. I know."

"Well, Erdmann would say it's scarcity that makes it profitable to be a pusher."

"In a way that's true. Right now it pays people to, um, make converts. But, see, dear, that's not the whole story. If you had a substance that some people wanted and you made it harder to get, the price would go up. Sure it would. And it would pay people to supply it. But you see, underlying that is the admission that people *do* want it. The trouble with drugs is that they're very attractive. Lots of people want them. If you just let them be sold anywhere—every magazine rack and candy counter—plenty of people would buy them who don't buy them now. People who don't right now because they're afraid to do something illegal."

"They say you'd cut out organized crime."

"Oh, sure you would." She patted my hand. Then she held out a package of mints, and I took one. "But how would that help if you have the country addicted? How's it going to make it better just to call it legal? It's still bad for people. You'd still have people's health destroyed. I see the effects right here. My fourth-graders, they come from families—I couldn't even tell you some of the things. Their mothers get high and wander away. There's nobody in the house to take care of them. Heat goes off in the house. Food runs out. Come to school in the same clothes all week and been eating nothing but potato chips and Coca-Cola! Or not eating at all. I'm supposed to get them interested in spelling!"

"Well, I suppose Louise—"

"It's like a plague. It's a plague worse than bubonic plague. It's worse than AIDS. I don't think we'll ever stamp it out, but we can quarantine it. Isolate the pushers. Get them in jail. Jail the importers."

"But can you ever get ahead of it?"

"I don't know. But maybe we can keep up with it. You know the old saying about eternal vigilance? I'd like *much* stronger drug laws. Much stiffer penalties. You know, anybody who buys drugs is contributing to the death of somebody, somewhere. They're nothing but murderers."

"Louise—"

"Louise was as bad as somebody carrying the plague, going around sneezing and coughing on us all!"

WHEN YOSEMITE SAM had arrived that morning, Mike was still sleeping. But he was sleeping naturally, not thrashing and gasping for breath, as he had done in the night. His bad dreams had kept me awake, because I didn't dare close my door and not hear him. For all I knew, he might take it into his head to get up and run out into the street. Sam had said no, that the stage for that had passed, but who really could be sure?

My head ached when I got out of bed. Two cups of coffee helped. Also a yogurt. Having eaten a plain yogurt made me feel virtuous, so I ate a sugared doughnut, too. I know an emergency when I see one.

Mike had looked quiet by then, so I took his clothes and mine to the laundromat, the Wishee Washee, on the corner. Went back and checked him. Went back and put the clothes through a complete wash cycle a second time. They needed it. Checked Mike. Went back and put them in the dryer. Checked Mike. Went back and picked up the clothes. Each time I checked Mike, I ate just a little something. You have to keep up your strength if you missed sleep.

At eleven, when Yosemite arrived, he promised to dress Mike and take him to the meeting. And lock the door on the way out.

So when I finished with Leota Parks at twelve-thirty, I had the whole day left. Leota Parks was a puzzle to me. She clearly hated Louise Sugarman. Despite her insistence that she disliked what she considered Louise's trading on her appearance, it had the flavor of personal dislike. She probably had a family member destroyed by drugs. But did that mean she would actually kill Louise?

One thing for sure: She had a clear appraisal that it was Louise's persona that gave repeal in Illinois a chance. No Louise, no repeal, at least not for years.

WITH TIME AVAILABLE, it seemed like checking out PASA headquarters—Parents Against Substance Abuse—was a good idea. Ben Hoskinson may be my uncle (or my aunt's cousin), but that didn't make him a saint. For all anyone knew, he might hate Louise Sugarman as much as Leota Parks did.

But he wasn't there, even though it was only early afternoon. Torkel Gates was.

There were posters on all the walls. "Just Say No." Personally, I like that one. It assumes that people have some sense.

Torkel stood under a poster of a monkey. It was either a monkey that you were supposed to get off your back or the monkey that would rather use cocaine than eat. But the way Torkel was standing, the monkey peeked over him like a second head. Torkel's reddish nose was redder than ever.

"Do you have a cold?" I asked.

"Allergies." Torkel was never a big talker. He carried a broom and a large green plastic bag. He's the person at PASA who keeps the mess from taking over.

"Uncle Ben out for lunch?"

"Home. Didn't feel well."

"Oh, okay. See you."

He unbent a little. After all, the last time he saw me, I must have been leaving feet first on a stretcher and covered with blood and brains.

"You feeling better?" he said.

"Oh, sure. Don't I *look* better?"

His answer left me wondering about him. He said, "I guess."

NOT WANTING TO LET the grass grow under my feet, though there is precious little grass at Lincoln and Halsted, I decided to walk the mile and a half to the Common Sense headquarters and then go to Uncle Ben's apartment on my way back to my place.

There were posters at Common Sense, too.

The young man at the front desk was still there.

"I've come to stuff envelopes," I told him.

"They're stuffed."

"Oh."

"But you could run them through the meter. And say, you look a lot better!"

"Thanks."

I metered for an hour. As I did so, I studied the layout. Back where the tearful young woman had gone the last time I had been there, I saw two doors. Each door was glass. One was lighted; one was not.

After a time, the young woman I had seen before came up a stairway from the basement. She gave me some shallow boxes for the mailings. Then she went into the darkened office and came out with some papers. She took them into the lighted office. There were mumblings in a man's voice and responses in a woman's voice. Then she came out empty-handed and went downstairs again.

I finished my task. The young man at the front desk got up, locked his drawer, petty cash, no doubt, took his jacket, and went to the front door. "Want a doughnut?" he asked.

I did, but I said, "No, thanks."

As the door closed behind him, I pushed aside the mailings.

I knocked on the lighted office.

"Come in," the man's voice said.

I did. It was Max Sugarman.

He smiled. He had a very pleasant smile.

"I stopped to talk with you at the funeral—" I began.

"Yes, I remember. Your name was—um—"

"Catherine Marsala."

"Of course. Yes. Um?"

"I think I mentioned that Ms. Sugarman had offered to give me an interview. I'm so sorry that it can't ever take place. But I'm still doing an article on her."

"That's good. That's good. It's a great blessing you survived, at least."

Would I say that if someone I loved had been blown away? Or would I think, I wish you'd sat between her and the bomb. Well, he couldn't say *that* even if he thought it.

Of course, everything else being equal, the husband is the first suspect. In terms of the number of motives, he had more possibles than anyone else—possible personal hatred, possible envy of her success, possible financial benefit from her death, possible wish to take over at Common Sense. With my favorite suspect gone, my job was to *cherchez l'homme* without being obvious at it.

"How will Common Sense get along without her?" I asked.

"Not very well. Not very well. She was the heart and soul of this organization."

Max Sugarman had a slightly singsong intonation and a melancholy way of talking, which was probably habitual, not circumstance. People who have sprightly voices tend to have sprightly voices even at funerals. Max had most likely spoken this way all his life. He would surely not be capable of the bright, entertaining platform speech, as Louise was.

"What did she think the chances were for repeal?"

"Very good. Very good," he said mournfully.

"Did she have the votes in Springfield?"

"Not a majority yet. No. But she had enough to make a very serious showing. A very serious showing."

"Ah. And she thought it would grow in later votes?"

"Well, actually, she thought she could build her base farther in time for this vote. She had some information—"

There was a knock on the door, and the young man stepped in on the heels of his knock.

"—something rather disreputable about one of our opposition." His vague eyes caught sight of the chap in the doorway. "Rufe. Doughnuts?"

"Uh-huh. I brought one back for you, too," Rufe said, looking at me, "but when I didn't see you, I thought you'd gone."

His eyes told me he knew I'd intentionally slipped in here in his absence. But he saw that Sugarman was talking with me, and he did not object. Sugarman got up.

"Have some coffee with us, Miss Marsala."

"Are you a mind reader?" I said to Rufe. "I did want one, but I didn't want to ask."

"A part-time mind reader."

We trooped to the urn in the front room. "What do I owe you?" I asked him.

"Nothing. Our vast petty cash runs to a doughnut for anyone who helps out. Mandy!" he shouted down the stairs.

Rufe poured coffee for four. He brought nondairy creamer and little sugar packets to the table. We three settled around the stamped bins of mailings. Mandy came upstairs. She carried a huge pile of some very dusty computer printout. I glanced at it as she put it down on the end of the table. Addresses. Thousands and thousands of addresses.

Rufe gave Max the coffee creamer and sugar. Mandy got up and got him a plastic spoon to stir with. Rufe took out a doughnut, butterscotch frosted with pecans, put it on a paper napkin, and slid it over in front of Max. Then he dumped the remaining three on a spread-out paper napkin. One Bismarck, one plump glazed doughnut, one jelly filled.

"My next miracle of mind reading. I'm going to bet you like glazed doughnuts," Rufe told me.

"You're right!" I said in tones of amazement.

"Mandy likes jelly, and I like Bismarcks." He pushed them around appropriately.

I didn't tell him I also liked jelly filled and Bismarcks. Why blow a pleasant relationship?

"What will Common Sense do now?"

"We have a lot of supporters," Max said mournfully.

At the same time, Rufe said, "Regroup and forge on."

I looked at Mandy for her words on the subject.

She was staring at Max Sugarman, and a teardrop had made its way down her cheek and into a cerise smear of jelly on her upper lip.

Once or twice during that rather gloomy afternoon snack, I saw Mandy catch Rufe's eye, or vice-versa, as Max Sugarman made some statement. They were worried. I felt like an intruder. This was no place for hard-hitting journalism. After some ten minutes I got up to go.

"I'll be back when I can," I said cheerily.

Max walked me to the door. His tall, thin body drooped attentively toward me. "What would Mrs. Sugarman have done with that information?" I asked when I thought we were out of earshot of Mandy and Rufe.

"What inf— Oh, about the opposition."

"Would she have forced somebody to back down? Behind the scenes?"

"Oh, no!" He was aghast. "That would be blackmail."

"Mmm. Well—"

"She would have spoken out about it. Gone to the media. She was always entirely up-front."

"What will *you* do with it?"

"I can't do anything with it. I don't know what it was."

NINE

IT WAS NOW FOUR-THIRTY. On impulse, I went to a phone booth on State Street. By sheer luck there was still a phone book in the booth. When your luck is in, it's in. The second piece of luck: Leota Parks had a number listed under her own name. Her address was west of downtown, but not too far. I picked up my car and drove over.

The neighborhood was near the Madison Street area that was burned during the riots in 1968. Her block was intact and well maintained.

The buildings, though, were disheartening. Built four stories, the precise limit beyond which city codes require an elevator, they were cheaply made, wood frame faced with that stuff that is intended to look like brick but in fact looks like coffee grounds glued to tar paper. The backs of the apartments have wooden porches and stairs that are pulling loose from the walls. The porches are littered with mattresses, potted plants, and laundry.

I pulled up and got out of the car. Three tiny black children, girls, were playing on the front walk of the house. They had a wicker doll carriage that had lost much of its white paint over the years. Inside was a cloth doll that had lost most of her clothes.

I said, "Good afternoon."

They stared at me and one said, "Hello," shyly.

Parks was the second floor. I rang. A window opened, and Leota Parks stared out at me, then said, "Come on up."

It was a large apartment, running from the front of the building to the back, but cramped with furniture and objects. There were toys, girl's clothing, another baby carriage, several dolls, cacti, a philodendron, and some school books in the living room.

"I forgot to ask you something," I said to Leota Parks.

She smiled indulgently and said, "Sure, honey."

A girl of about twelve came out of the hall. Leota said, "Ms. Marsala, this is my granddaughter, Maleka."

Maleka said, "How do you do?" So did I.

Leota Parks said, "Honey, would you get Ms. Marsala and me a glass of Coke?" Maleka left.

I heard a key at the door. A girl of about eight or nine entered carrying two large, flat books that looked like history or civics to me. Her hair was held in tufts by red ribbons, and she wore a red plaid dress. Someday she would be a really gorgeous woman.

"My granddaughter Selena," said Leota. "Ms. Marsala," she said to Selena.

"My name is Cat," I said.

The Coke arrived. I thanked Maleka. Maleka asked Leota whether she should start the rice. Leota said yes. I was feeling more and more uncomfortable. Ms. Parks could probably see right through me. My intent had been to try to discover whether Leota Parks had a family member on drugs, and unfortunately it was all too embarrassingly evident. Where was the mother or father of these children, Leota's daughter or son?

"Now, honey," said Leota, "you know you didn't have any questions, so don't upset your head making a few up. You wanted to see how I lived."

"I should have known better than to try to fool a grade-school teacher."

She started to laugh. "I can tell who's hiding the bubble gum in his cheek, that's for sure!"

The little girl who had been playing doll in front came in, along with a girl about two years older, possibly seven.

"Isn't that door locked, child?" Leota said, and introduced us. "Put the homework in your room and start setting the table."

In the same breath she said to me, "I guess we got all girl genes in our family."

"Your daughter's children?"

"Mmm-mm. You want to know how drugs affect a family? Okay. Here it is, right here. I got five girl children to raise on a teacher's salary."

"I know how drugs affect a family," I said. "My brother's in prison for drugs."

Her face went through three expressions. The first was one I'd seen before, which is something like "White girl, you don't know the half." I never know what to do about that one. Saying you've got troubles, too, doesn't really help. Anyway, within a second she looked slightly disbelieving—was I trying to grab her sympathy?—and then, knowing it was true, a look of pity overcame everything else. She put her arm around me.

"Well, girl, I know, I know, I know," she said. And I was sure she did know.

I HAD INTENDED TO GO to Uncle Ben's, but I found that I couldn't do one more interview that day if my life depended on it. And there was no particular reason at that point to think it did. By now it was past six-thirty. I slogged toward home from the street where I was lucky enough to find a parking place, stopping off only briefly at the dry cleaners and thinking about the sense of defeat hanging over the Common Sense office.

It wasn't quite the defeat of the organization itself. They could probably rally support. It was Max Sugarman. He was temporarily in charge, and obviously Rufe and Mandy believed that meant nobody was in charge. Even his wife had not trusted him with explosive information. How subtly the mind works! She may have been entirely right in protecting him. After all, *he* hadn't been blown up.

Probably the insiders were trying to think of a way of replacing him without hurting his feelings.

By the time I trudged up my block, under the el, in the tiny lobby, and up the stairs, I could hardly hold my head up. The pressure at the back of my skull had come back. Not quite a headache yet, but something back there was getting ready to dig in its claws.

I didn't see Mike until I stepped on him.

Slight exaggeration. I stepped on a paper bag next to him.

"Hey!" he said. "That's dinner!"

"Oh, boy, could I use it!"

MIKE WAS CONTRITE. Knowing him as well as I did, the contrition would be expected to last between one and a half and three days. Knowing me as well as he did, he expressed his contrition by bringing food.

What I had stepped on was the bag of egg rolls. But they are just as good flat. Nothing had actually oozed out. We turned on the oven and popped everything in to warm. Meanwhile, Mike made tea. He didn't say anything specifically about the fact that he was making tea and not looking for beer, but he didn't really have to. I didn't refer to it, either. Yosemite Sam had made it clear to me more than once before that nagging didn't help. Making excuses for him didn't help. Threats didn't help. Helping didn't help.

What would help in the long run, according to Sam, was Mike's own ability to realize he had a disease. And for friends to lay off the subject. But to remain friends.

Okay, I could remain friends.

Mike had brought orange-peel beef, tofu with mushrooms, chicken pea pod, and a big tub of rice, as well as the egg rolls. All my favorites. "What! No sweet-and-sour soup?" I asked, but he must have known I was kidding. He grabbed a can of Redi-wip from the refrigerator and tried to spray me.

I ducked in time, so he sprayed my egg roll.

"That isn't bad," I said, tasting it. It ran off the hot egg roll pretty fast, anyway.

"We'll leave everything else in the oven until we want it," he said.

"Good thinking. What would you have done if I hadn't come home? Sat there all night with cold Chinese food?"

"Sure. Got here at six, figured it couldn't spoil before eight. If you weren't here by seven-thirty, I'd go home and eat it myself."

"All of it?"

"Half tonight, half tomorrow, in my lonely bachelor pad."

Long John Silver was in my bedroom. I often moved his cage in there when I was going to be out all day. I'd leave the cage door open so he could fly around but close my bedroom door so he didn't have the run of the living room and kitchen. Especially the kitchen. He once tried to eat a Brillo pad.

Long John came swooping and *Braaak!*ing into the living room. Mike was bringing in the Chinese food.

"*Gaah!* Why do you let that thing stay loose in your bedroom?"

"It's only fair he get some space."

"Doesn't he poop bird droppings on the bed?"

"No, I have a perch in there for him. I put newspapers under the perch."

Long John perched on Mike's shoulder.

"He certainly isn't decorative," Mike said, twitching his shoulder while balancing dinner plates.

LJ is a West African gray parrot, or *Psittacus erithacus* for short. They are a sort of gunmetal color with splotches of rusty red, about the shade of dried blood. "Gray parrots are not the best lookers; they're the best talkers."

"Call me Ishmael! *Awk!*" said LJ.

"It's not morally right to keep birds confined," said Mike.

"Watch it! He likes pea pods!"

"Scat! Scram!"

"*Awk!* Prophet! Thing of evil!"

"I didn't imprison him," I said. "By the time I got him, he was used to house living. For that matter, he's not even an illegal, imported parrot—he came in before the import laws. He was owned by an English professor from Northwest University. The English teacher lived in the apartment downstairs, where Mr. Ederle is now, and he had to move to Alberta, though I'm not at all sure why. Something to do with a woman. And he wanted somebody kind and responsible to take LJ."

"But you said you'd do it, anyway?"

"And the English prof, Dr. Regnery, had taken LJ after LJ's previous owner, Pierre LeChoux, who used to live *up*stairs, who had been a creole chef in New Orleans, and who got LJ from an uncle who was a shrimp trawler, that is, he ran a shrimp trawler—put a lid over the rice or he'll eat it!— had died and left him an orphan. LJ, that is."

"Good God! How old is this bird?"

"We never knew. We don't know who had him before that. At least forty."

Mike looked at LJ with a respect he had never shown before.

"Older than I am?"

"Yup."

"I think it's unnaturally cannibalistic the way he's eyeing the chicken."

"It's the pea pods."

"How would parrot with pea pods taste?"

"Mike!"

By an association of ideas, Mike started to tell me about a new feature he had just thought of.

"Petting zoos," he said. "The little zoo-within-a-zoo where kids can pet young animals?"

"So?"

"Did you know that most of those animals are superfluous? They kill them when they get too old to be cute?"

"They don't!"

"Oh, yes, they do. Not the valuable animals, like goril-
las. But the baby goats and some of the lambs and so on."

"Why can't they put them in the zoo?"

"Overcrowding."

"Give them to other zoos?"

"They have enough already."

"Set them free?"

"Where? They're hand raised and don't know how to live
in the wild. They'd just be slaughtered."

"Oh."

"See, I'm going to do an exposé on how the petting zoos
are based on something not so cute and on what the effect
of working in them is on the employees. Total human interest!"

"Do you have a solution to offer?"

"No. Not really."

"You need one."

"Not necessarily. Not for an exposé."

"There is a solution. Birth control for the animals."

"Sure. But then there wouldn't be babies for the petting
zoos."

"I see."

"It's going to be great. Don't you think so? Best thing
I've ever done?"

"Mike, what about your article on judges? Wasn't Bernie expecting that?"

"He likes this one. Come on. Tell me this'll be great!"

"It'll be great! But what about the judges?"

"Oh, I've dropped that for now. Not exciting enough."

I sighed. Mike would never be able to settle down.

WE ATE EVERY BIT of the dinner. Every grain of rice, except
for what LJ grabbed. This put me in a far better mood than
I had been in when I came home. I started to tell Mike about
the case.

"TORKEL GATES SOUNDS suspicious to me," Mike said about twenty minutes later.

"Why?"

"Oh, the ignored factotum. Quiet, unappreciated assistant following his master loyally around. No glory. No name in the papers."

"But what would he gain by killing Uncle Ben's enemy, if you could call Louise Uncle Ben's enemy? Surely not a Becket thing—somebody rid me of this meddlesome Louise?"

"Well, if later on—say, next month—your Uncle Ben got run over by a cement mixer, that would leave Torkel in charge."

"Oh, really! Actually, for all we know, it might leave Aunt Elise in charge. Or some other assistant. I'm not sure. Be serious, Mike!"

"All right. Being perfectly serious. The people who hated Louise Sugarman, or hated her beliefs, which for the moment we'll take as the same thing, are—?"

"Uncle Ben and Aunt Elise. No, leave out Elise. She wasn't there. Torkel. Leota Parks. Glen Barton—he's from the Drug Enforcement Administration—"

"Okay."

"And Lt. Stan Gotchka. He's in charge of the drug squad for the Chicago Police Department. Uncle Ben, Glen Barton, Leota Parks, and Stan Gotchka were the four who were going to speak in favor of the existing laws. Or even stronger laws, I suppose."

"And they balanced the program with four antis?"

"Pro-repeal, they're called. There were only three of them. Professor Robert Erdmann, the economist. Dr. Cameron Lloyd, a psychiatrist. I haven't talked with him yet. Louise, of course. And there was also Charles Jaffee."

"Old Gentleman Joe's kid?"

"Well, yes. If you put it that way."

"What was he doing? Was he pro-repeal?"

"No, neutral. He was going to talk about treatment centers. I guess his father's foundation's established treatment centers."

"Gee! American enterprise in action. Just like the robber barons whose sons founded hospitals. Cure the diseases caused by the factories that made their fortunes."

"What do you mean?"

"The factories were unsafe, unventilated—"

"No. Jaffee."

"Well, he must have imported drugs in the bad old days, mustn't he? Before he got religion."

"I suppose. Forget that for now." I would just as soon not talk about Charlie Jaffee with Mike. I'd straighten out my ideas on that later.

"One neutral. Three pro-repeal and four pro-laws. It hardly seems fair."

"Fair enough. The organizers of the symposium may have wanted to seem mildly in favor of antidrug laws but reasonable."

Mike was a people person. Not terribly analytical, not legalistic, not a numbers person.

"You know," he said, "there are two categories of people who can really resent a prominent leader like Louise Sugarman."

"Go ahead."

"You've been thinking of people who hated her point of view. That's one category. People who detest her and everything she stands for."

"Leota Parks."

"And your Uncle Ben, and your Lt. Gotchka, possibly. Maybe even Glen Barton."

"Maybe."

"The other category is people who agree with her, who've always taken the public position she takes and who just haven't got as far with it. She has the name and the game and the fame."

"Erdmann? Dr. Lloyd?"

"And Max Sugarman."

"No, never! Not Sugarman. He's too ineffectual. Mike, you should see him. He forgets where the sugar for the coffee is. They're wondering how to ease him out. If I have *any* ability to watch facial reactions and tell what they mean, the people at Common Sense are wondering what in hell they're going to do with him."

"That doesn't tell you how he feels about it. He may have resented Louise's power for years."

"And her ease in speaking to crowds," I said.

"And the fact that lots of people loved her."

"Yes, I suppose. But I don't believe it."

"Then there's Erdmann. With Louise gone, he could step into her shoes. He's well known. He's the likely heir."

"He's very—um—abrasive."

"I didn't say he would do the job as well as she did. I said he was the likely heir. And then there's Lloyd. He's reasonably well known. I think he's less well suited to running an organization, but he's a good public speaker. Likable. Shares that ability with Louise. I heard him at the press club last March."

"I've seen him. But never talked with him."

"If there's a dark horse in the list, he's it."

I thought about the two slender triple A batteries and the tiny switch and light. All rigged, they would make a thin cylinder. It would be maybe just a little fatter than a cigarette. Encased in paper, it might look like a cigarette.

I thought about Leota Parks and her totem-pole necklace. Dr. Lloyd and the rolled sheets of paper he was chewing on. And somebody had one of those fat, big red pens. Erdmann. Cigarette holders? No, I would have noticed that. Cigars, cigarillos, pipes?

WE SNUGGLED UP on the sofa and watched some television. *Passage to Marseilles* was on. Flashbacks within flashbacks.

When we broke for popcorn, Mike said, "I'm sorry about last night."

"Oh, well, that's okay."

"No, it's not. You know, my grandfather was an alcoholic. And so is my older brother."

"Al?"

"Yeah. Dad's a teetotaler. He probably has the genes for alcoholism. If they're right about it being hereditary. But he was so scared by his father's behavior—"

"Right."

"Sometimes I think I may have a drinking problem."

"Drinking problem," not "alcoholic."

Halfway there, I guess. According to Yosemite Sam, if they can't say it, they're not at the bottom and ready to start on the long road back up.

TEN

EVERY OTHER THURSDAY, I visit my brother. Teddy was always my favorite brother. The youngest, the shortest, the most vulnerable of them all, he was never able to stand up to my father the way some of the others did or just quietly go his way, either. When he disagreed with Dad, he just couldn't resist saying so, and then he had to take the consequences.

I visited him because I knew Dad wouldn't, because Mom would when she could, but it was hard for her, because I knew my brothers would only sporadically, and because I loved him best of all.

This particular Thursday I had a lot to do. A great deal of the research you do on any piece you write is just telephoning sources. It sounds simple, but it is extremely time consuming. People are out. People don't know what you want, but they give you another name. You call that name, and the person can't figure out why anybody ever thought he would know what you needed.

Point is: I had to do the whole-hog vacuum-cleaner imitation today. Suck up dirt as fast as I could.

Therefore, to squeeze my visit to Teddy in, I popped into my car at six A.M. It was two hours to Granite Ridge, where Granite Ridge Correctional Center was located. It is a medium-security prison, not far from the Illinois/Iowa state line.

Through Chicago the traffic was heavy. Rush hour starts early in these parts. Lasts late. In fact, we'd be better off forgetting about the notion of rush hour and calling a brief period during the night the quiet hour.

West of Chicago, as soon as the densely packed factories
trail off into "industrial corridors" and shopping malls trail
off into an occasional convenience store, you are in cornfields. These cornfields stretch away across Illinois, across
Iowa, across Nebraska, to the Colorado border, seven
hundred miles of corn.

It was September, and some of the fields of early sweet
corn were already in stubble. Their rounded, bristly cheeks
contrasted with the bearded miles of field corn, kernels still
drying and hardening on brown stalks. Birds were flocking
up on the telephone wires. Little birds, the first to go south
because they lived on insects. The geese would come through
later, trailing in loose vees like seaweed through the sky,
scavenging scattered corn in the fields in the early morn-
ings.

And Teddy? Would he see them pass overhead?

They would go south, and he would be unable to follow.
He would see them go south next year again and be unable
to follow. And the next year. And the next.

Two hours and a stop at a Stucky's for coffee later, I
pulled into the visitor's lot at Granite. Eighteen-foot-high
woven wire fence surrounds the compound. At the top of
the fence is an endless roll of barbed wire. Inside the fence
is a wide, flat yard of immaculate grass, barbered and
weeded, not a gum wrapper on its surface. Lots of free labor, I thought.

Not a bush on its surface to hide behind, either.

Through this barricade protrudes the red-brick entrance
to the visitor's center.

I walked up to the doors and stood there while the guard
inside took a look at me. Since I had no submachine gun in
evidence, nor was I backed up by any bunch of guys in
stocking masks carrying Uzis, he buzzed the door, and I
opened it.

"Good morning!" I said to the guard at the desk. He
knew me from before.

"Cold out?" he asked.

Cold in, I thought, but I said, "No. Still nice," and handed him my driver's license. Despite the dozens of times he had seen me, I knew the license number would be punched into a machine on the wall that would check for outstanding warrants on me.

Meanwhile, I grabbed the clipboard with the visitor's sign-in. I wrote my prisoner's name, Theodore Marsala, his number, which was L05168, my name, my address, my driver's license number, my social security number, my phone number, my number's number (just kidding), my relationship to the prisoner. I wrote "sister." The person ahead of me had written "Granny." The one before her had written "fiend."

They gave me a key to a locker. I stored my dangerous items, like my two dozen pens and pencils, my potential drug-smuggling item (a down vest), and all money but a ten-dollar bill. The sign on the wall listed other prohibited objects: any opened cigarette package, books, magazines, newspapers, medications, anything metal, more than one baby diaper, and children's toys. Had I brought a bomb or an Uzi, this was the place to leave it.

Then I sat down to wait. And wait. I had got there ahead of the "count," which is important. The count is not a meticulously tailored gentleman from Transylvania but a period of forty-five minutes that takes place eight times a day. During the count, guards actually physically count *by sight* every inmate in the place. If you get in to see your prisoner before the count takes place, he is counted in the visitor's canteen. But if you get there just before a count, you wait the forty-five minutes in addition to the half hour or so it takes them to get your inmate for you, anyhow.

Teddy, inside, would be running through a full strip search to come to the visitor's canteen. I felt so sorry for him that I always sank into sloughs of guilt when I became impatient at just plain sitting and waiting.

After twenty minutes, a female guard called me into the visitor's search room. To enter it, I passed through a metal detector. In the search room, knowing the procedure, I slipped off my shoes, showed her the bottoms of my feet, raised my arms so she could pat me down, and leaned my head forward so she could check in my hair. Today she didn't look under my tongue. Sometimes they do; sometimes they don't.

She stamped my hand with dye that shows up under ultraviolet light.

From there I walked toward a barred double-glassed sliding door on a metal track. The woman who had searched me nodded. A guard in a bulletproof glass booth pushed a button that slid the door open. I entered an "air-lock" vestibule. The door slid shut behind me with a firm *thwack*. Three seconds passed. Only then did the door on the far side open and let me out.

I walked into the canteen.

You've seen movies in which pining gun molls visit their desperado husbands in prison and sit on one side of a glass panel, communicating by telephone? Or one on each side of a woven-wire barricade, where they hold hands—I mean fingertips—by clutching at the wire?

Not in Illinois. The room you meet in looks like a featureless McDonald's. It has bright orange molded-plastic hamburger-joint chairs permanently bolted to metal arms under blue-plastic tables. If you wanted to pile up chairs to form a barricade against the guards, you have no material. At one end of the room is a food-service unit—read radar range and refrigerator. There are two inmates who run it. They are the only inmates who are allowed to touch money. They will microwave preformed, prebunned hamburgers for you or unfreeze frozen pizza, and they sell candy bars and soda pop. In other words, you get your four basic food groups: sugar, fat, salt, and preservatives.

I bought Teddy two Milky Way candy bars. They were his favorite, and he could not get them inside the prison.

There is a booth with one-way glass high in the wall. Inside the booth are guards watching the room. Two other guards, one male and one female, stroll around the canteen and assign you seats and keep watch. I was assigned table 22.

I waited.

Teddy came in wearing blue denim. On him it looks good. He has curly red hair and freckles.

Teddy is twenty-three, twelve years younger than I am. Therefore, I try very hard not to mother him.

But I hug him.

"Lookin' good, Cat." Teddy had one arrest for possession of marijuana at the age of twenty-one. An adult conviction. When he was found with PCP two years later, it was a second conviction. The judge threw the book at him. Teddy seems clearheaded today. For a while after his arrest he was mentally mashed potato, and he still has periods of confusion and memory lapses.

"You're looking okay yourself." I wouldn't have said it just to flatter him. The only way I could handle the pain of it, when Teddy was first imprisoned, was to make him absolutely special to me. I decided he would be the one person in all the world I was always completely open with. No barriers. No bravado.

It wasn't such a big leap. We had always been close, but until then I had sometimes told him what I thought he ought to hear—motherlike—or tried to be the big, successful sister. Ha!

"So how's Dad?" he asked.

"Well, actually, I haven't seen him since I was here last."

"How about Mom?" He was unwrapping the first of the Milky Way bars. He knew they were for him without asking.

"I had lunch with her last week. She's—um—like always."

"Like how do you mean?"

"You know. Wearing her old cloth coat. You buy her lunch, she says, 'I can just order a salad. I can have something quick. I know you're busy.'"

He grinned.

"Then you go to dessert," I said, "and she says, 'Oh, I don't need dessert. You know I never eat desserts, Catherine. I'm used to starting on the dishes while everybody else is finishing.'"

He smiled more sadly. "Cat, how do we get to the be the way we are?"

"Figure it out and you'll be the new guru."

"Man, I don't want to be anybody's guru. If I can manage myself, that's good enough for me."

"You sound good."

"I'm not saying, 'Hey, you look familiar, lady, but what's your name?'"

"Right."

"Cat, I've been thinking."

"Bad news, Charlie." This was an old catchphrase for us. Like a lot of the things that cause kids to break up with laughter, it had never meant anything, except that it was *ours*. We started laughing now. Loudly. We leaned on the table and laughed. Probably the reason we laughed was simply delight that we could, under the circumstances. The guard looked at us, but he smiled. Sometimes they do.

"What do you like about your job?"

I hesitated. The basic answer was one I hardly wanted to say to him in this place. But I had resolved on honesty.

"Freedom," I said.

"Okay. Is that all?"

"No. It lets me do a lot of different things. Book research. Meeting a wide range of people. Drive around town with a purpose and feel like a hell of a real person. It's a job people envy. Of course, they don't see the drawbacks."

"What are they?"

"Low pay. The average freelance writer makes an income that's below the official U.S. poverty line."

"And?"

"You can't coast. There are days when it's cold or raining and Chicago looks like it's made of damp gray clay. And

I have to go out and trudge around and dredge up some exciting facts by sheer willpower. Why do you want to know?''

"Well, I was thinking what I'll do when I get out."

"I imagine a person could do a lot of that kind of thinking in here."

"Yup. It's a problem, because a lot of businesses won't hire you. And a lot of jobs I might have liked are out."

"Like what?"

"Oh, I'll never get into law school. That kind of thing."

"Mmm. Okay."

"So I need something where I can prove myself."

"And so?"

"I thought I might want to be a freelance writer."

Oh, hell. Oh, wow. He wants to be like his older sister. "I'm honored," I whispered.

He nodded, smiling. "You should be. See, I figure if I write something good, they'll buy it and not care what my background has been."

"That's true, by and large. But, Ted, it isn't very secure."

"What is?"

"Come on. There are secure jobs. Oh, never mind. I'll tell you what. Do they have courses in writing?"

"The DOC courses are pretty much a joke. This is no correctional center. It's a storage center."

"All right. Forget that. What I'm going to do is this. I take all the major papers in Chicago, most of the major magazines, and a lot of the minor ones. I'll pick out half a dozen of the most typical—one of each kind of thing, news, glossy, specialty, whatever—and send you a subscription. Then you read 'em and you psych 'em out. What they like. What they print. What they don't print. How they structure it. That's really the way to do it, anyhow. Journalism courses teach you the obvious. Then you pick an issue and write a three-page article on it and send it to me. I'll give you a critique. Okay?"

"Okay!"

"But listen, I'm vicious when I criticize. I'll tell you everything that's wrong."

"Sure."

"Idle compliments won't help you. What you'll get is absolutely no bullshit."

"Okay!"

AFTER TWO HOURS I had to leave. For one thing, I had a long drive back and a lot of work to do this afternoon. And I was going to watch Uncle Ben do his thing tonight at a school. Besides, after two hours those plastic seats ruin your sacroiliac.

I said good-bye to Teddy and got mentally ready to leave him alone in that place. "You're sounding a lot better."

"Well, I'm off the stuff."

"What about when you get out?"

"What do you mean?"

"When you can get the stuff again."

"Are you kidding? That's not why I'm off it."

"Huh?"

"I can get it here."

"How?"

"The guards smuggle it in and sell it."

Oh.

I said, "Well, then why aren't you using?"

"I don't know. It's like—here—it's the opposite of home, you know, Cat? Here they expect me to want it. It would kind of satisfy them. Confirm something. You know what I mean?"

"You don't want to give them the satisfaction?"

"Yeah."

"But you don't mean— Are you saying Dad's expectations for you were too high?"

"No, that wasn't it. I think he expected me to screw up. It was just that he was pushing me all the time. Everything had to be done his way. I guess at a certain age you feel like showing you can't just be pushed around."

"I know."

"Yeah, I know you know."

THE AFTERNOON WAS paper work. Making notes. Filing. Raiding files.

A friend of mine named Stinky, who is fourteen years of age, has helped me put my computer and modem to use. Fourteen, of course, is the age to look for if you want somebody who plays the computer like Heifetz plays the violin. Kids of that age computed before they spoke. They were on their third generation of computers before they graduated from school.

Anyway, keeping this description nonspecific so as not to bring retaliation down on my head, I have two main methods of access to information: friends and my computer. One way or the other, I get information from the Department of Motor Vehicles, the National Crime Information Center computer, the Auto Title Department, the Department of Corrections, and half a dozen more.

Some of the various trailers I had put out had caught information.

Cars can tell you quite a bit about a person. I like to actually look at a person's car if I want to understand him or her. What make is it? Is it full of trash? It is spotlessly clean? Does he keep emergency items in it? Food? Clothes? At this stage, however, with seven people as suspects, I was just going for the basics.

Glen Barton, the DEA chap, drove a dark blue Ford, this year's, owned by the federal government.

Leota Parks had a 1974 brown Chevy, which she had bought used in 1981. She had been ticketed for a muffler violation in 1983 and twice for lights not working in 1986 and 1987.

Dr. Cameron Lloyd, the psychiatrist, owned a tan 1984 VW. No tickets.

Professor Robert Erdmann had a red Porsche and a rebuilt Red T-bird. And dozens of tickets for speeding and double-parking. In fact, he seemed to keep just under the number of moving violations per year (three) that in Illinois will get your license taken away.

Lt. Stanley Gotchka had owned a white Ford Escort, but it had been repossessed within the last thirty days.

Uncle Ben's car I knew. He had a dark blue Lincoln Continental with dark blue leather upholstery. No tickets.

Torkel Gates was making payments on a Pinto, which should fall apart just about the time he got it paid for. No tickets.

Max Sugarman drove a four-year-old Buick. He had tickets for improper lane usage and failure to signal. But these were not associated with DUIs. In other words, he just forgot what he was doing.

ELEVEN

THERE WAS A DISCREET hum in the auditorium. I imagined that it was an angry hum, although you might not have assumed that if you'd just had an audio recording of it. It was the angry faces that told me.

Riversedge was one of those new suburbs. Twenty years ago it had been an apple orchard, the huge Olaf Swendon pig farm, and a flood plain leading down to the Fox River. Fifteen years ago it had been a "development." Now it was a bona fide Chicago suburb, with no lot under half an acre and what the real estate people call "desirable public schools." I was in the auditorium of the desirable public high school, a school that had lost two students to drugs in the last two weeks and was hopping mad.

Except that when I looked closer at the faces, what I saw was not just anger but anger thinly covering fear, like the expression of an inexperienced actor. What these two kids had died of wasn't heroin or crack but designer drugs. The upper-class stuff. Somebody had made it in his basement. And maybe he had made it wrong.

The fear came because nobody had the faintest idea how to stop it. These people had moved out here to be away from the reach of city crime, away from soot, from air pollution, from noise pollution. This was God's half acre. They didn't need to lock their doors in the daytime. Probably a lot of them didn't lock their doors at night. And here, where they were quite sure no thief or murderer would break in, death strolled in with their children—in their children's pockets.

And they didn't know why. And they could not get away.

I had come up with Uncle Ben. They had asked him to speak, and I wanted to see him in action, but I didn't expand on it, certainly not to the point of explaining it might give me a hint whether he would kill Louise Sugarman out of anger.

He said Aunt Elise had intended to be here, too, but some other meeting had come up. So we drove in my car, an indestructible black Ford Bronco, of which he did not approve. It was too muddy. Unwashed. Unkempt.

He sat now on the stage, looking distinguished in a three-piece suit. The school principal was talking. Another man sat on the stage near Uncle Ben. I had found a place in the rear corner of the audience.

"—sad occasion, when in the past we have come together on so many happy occasions. Still, there is cause to be hopeful in the fact that so many of us care and so many of us are willing to work together for the good of all. Now I want to give you Bissell Kendrick, the superintendent of schools."

There was spotty applause, the audience being divided between those who felt it was too sad an occasion to applaud and those who believed you had better be polite.

I listened to Kendrick with my ears and watched the faces in the audience with my eyes. People were attentive, but they had the sullen look of people who did not believe the problem was being solved.

"—counselors to deal with the grief and horror our students are feeling. Dr. Gorbim will visit each homeroom this week to speak and, during the remainder of his day, see students who feel the need to talk with him. This will be on a walk-in basis, and except for allowing the student ahead to finish, none will be turned away or left out—"

A woman near me with a teenager in tow was showing signs of increasing anger. Her face was red. She kept starting to raise her hand during pauses, then decided it wasn't the question period yet. The teenager, a boy who was painfully thin, leaned farther and farther away from her.

"—memorial service tomorrow—"

Two women were whispering a row in front of me. One of them kept shaking her head in negation. A man down my row sat with his arms crossed over his chest, his cheeks puffing in and out, in and out.

"—on all outsiders seen loitering in the area, and Chief Guilderson has promised me personally to make at least a visual inspection—"

One man near the front got up and walked out.

"—to introduce Ben Hoskinson, director of PASA, Parents Against Substance Abuse, who knows much more about the subject than I ever will."

Ben rose. So did the woman who had the teenage son. The son winced.

"Yes, ma'am," said the superintendent.

"About this counselor who will see our children if they go to his office. Will we as parents be informed if our child goes to see him?"

The kid nearly dislocated his neck leaning sideways, trying to disassociate himself from his mother. The superintendent was not pleased, either. But he had a way out.

"Um—Dr. Gorbim, how do you feel about that Dr.—You're here, aren't you? Dr. Gorbim?"

Gorbim rose. He had been seated in the second row. He turned to face the woman and most of the rest of the audience. "I'm a psychiatrist. I have always believed in maintaining confidentiality—"

"These are children! They're underage. If I took my child to a private psychiatrist, I would know he was seeing one—"

"If I am to be in the position to report on who comes to my office, it could be an unprofessional breach of ethics—"

"What if the child tells you he's using *drugs?*"

"Ma'am—"

"Excuse me!" Uncle Ben had stepped to the lectern. The superintendent turned to look at him, and there was a pause in the general rumble.

"I have a suggestion," said Uncle Ben. "We at PASA have found that whenever there is the slightest hint to teenagers that what they say or *even just their presence* at a counselor is going to be reported, they *don't go*. Now, you can probably find counselors who will report to parents. There are several who are doing that at different schools in the Chicago area, whatever the ethics of it. But let the kids hear it, let even *one child* report that his parents were informed, and your program will be useless. They won't go. I'm making a very simple point here. The choice is yours, not mine. But if you insist on disclosure, you will shoot your program in the foot. It's a question of whether you want things your way or whether you want them *effective*. My suggestion is that you think seriously about it for a few days before you decide to change Dr. Gorbim's plan. Let him do it his way for now."

By golly, the audience was quiet. Maybe I'd always thought of Uncle Ben as slightly feckless. Maybe when a person is a relative you don't give him much credit, like a prophet in his own country. But he had surely been effective here. Superintendent Kendrick knew when he was off the hook. He passed the baton to Ben instantly.

Ben began to speak.

"There is a plague sweeping our country. The plague of drugs. It is more insidious than AIDS, because people actually *choose* to become its victims. It is more subtle than the great epidemics of typhoid and the black death, because it takes many forms. Cocaine, crack, crank, heroin, amphetamines, poppers, marijuana, LSD, amyl nitrate, basement brew—if one is not available, they find another—"

This was a new Uncle Ben. Confident, authoritative. He looked healthier; his head, which usually fell down in front of his chest, was up and alert. His voice was clearer. He looked ten years younger.

I studied this change for a minute. He was *happy,* by golly, that's what it was. Up there on the stage with a message, he was happy.

"Just Say No programs are all very well. They really do work. But only for a certain number of kids. There are always a few who can't say no. Either because of the pressures of their lives or the failure of their parents to help them become people with confidence in themselves or because of economic factors that make them without hope—"

So here's my Uncle Ben transformed, and the question is: He loved it, would he kill to keep it? Did Louise Sugarman's program threaten what he loved most in life? Did he hate her?

"—ultimately is stopping the supply. There are two ways to do this. One is cutting off all routes of entry. That means better law enforcement at the borders. The second is seizing and destroying the drugs that get through or are produced in this country. And that means better policing. More surveillance of users. Better backtracking to the distributors. More effective informants.

"How do we achieve this? It's going to cost money, but it's worth it. We need an expert task force of policemen especially trained in drug traffic. This has to be an all-out war—local, state and federal. Write your local mayor and city councilmen. Write your state representatives and the governor. Write your senators and congressmen and the president! I have a sheet with addresses of all of those except your local officials, which I'm sure Superintendent Kendrick can supply—"

Someone got up in the first row. He held a stack of paper, and as I watched his back, he picked an inch-thick pile of sheets from the top and handed them to a woman at the end of the first row, who took one and passed the rest along. He went to the second row and handed out another inch. He turned, and I saw it was Torkel Gates.

Torkel must have driven out here by himself. Why didn't we ask him to ride with us? Did Uncle Ben treat him as a sort of slave, saying, "Pick up the flyers at the office and meet me at the auditorium at seven-thirty"? Did Torkel resent it? If so, why did he do it?

The end of the evening was the stuff that reporters love. Uncle Ben had given the dais to the chief of police, Ben having pretty much covered himself with glory. The chief, on the other hand, ran into trouble immediately. And why not, really, since he was the one who had both failed to head off the drug traffic that led to the two boys' deaths and failed to find the perpetrators afterward.

The man who had been puffing his cheeks in and out angrily rose from the crowd. He was big, and he was mad. "How do we know," he demanded, "that any of this stuff you're talking about is gonna work?"

And suddenly we had dozens on their feet.

There were questions shouted toward the stage and comments exchanged with people sitting nearby. The chief yelled something about needing more money for patrols and foot police to hang around the railroad station and small bus depot, and how was he supposed to do it on the budget he had, and then a woman with a voice piercing enough to carry above the din screamed, "Yes, but this stuff was made *right here!*"

Apparently this was true. Basement-chem-lab stuff. And they knew it, because half a dozen other people yelled, "What about that?" and, "Yeah!" and words to that effect. Then somebody on the stand, I think the chief, said, "If it's one of the kids here at the school—"

Everyone was yelling.

"Quiet!" Uncle Ben bellowed.

Hot damn! It worked. They were quiet enough, just barely, to listen to the chief.

"If this batch of chemicals was made by a kid here at the school," said the chief, "and it's not an outside pusher, then he will not be discovered by informants. We need people to come forward."

"Then what?"

"Then we can have the perpetrator prosecuted. This is homicide."

The quiet spread across the hall. I knew what they were thinking. It was one thing to string up an outside pusher, an outlander. It was quite another thing to send a local kid to prison for twenty years for a chemical error. Or life. Or—they were thinking—the death penalty. Felony murder. Kill him?

Uncle Ben said, calmly, into the quiet, "I know you're concerned with the tragedy that happened here this week. And that's understandable. But it's a mistake to get bogged down in the specific facts of these two sad deaths. The problem is bigger than that. The problem is the future.

"It's a question of commitment. Commitment of money and of responsibility. Of keeping watch and informing authorities—"

The meeting had been scheduled as "7:30 to 9:00." The superintendent rose and made "we've got to draw this to a close" noises. People began firing off solutions to the problem as if anything not spoken aloud would never be implemented.

One woman advocated that parents turn their child in to the police if they suspect he is using. "It's the only way to save them in the long run."

She got more cheers than boos.

An older woman suggested a small tax increase to be earmarked for a special local police task force. People yelled, "Okay!"

A man suggested a parents' network to exchange information. Somebody else yelled, "Easy to say, but who's going to set it up?" The man said he would, himself.

Knowing how things usually got at meetings, I diagnosed this as being very, *very* serious. People were willing not only to pay money but to do work. Putting their money and their time where their mouths were.

There were still shouted suggestions in the air when the superintendent said it was time to call a halt. The end of the meeting only differed from the meeting itself in that a lot of the audience stood up and started talking with their neighbors, and about a third of them surged up to the stage and milled and pushed around Uncle Ben and the police chief. I got out my pen and pad and asked questions.

"I noticed none of the speakers mentioned Louise Sugarman," I said to the older woman who had proposed the tax increase. She seemed practical and was not frothing at the mouth.

"Why would they?"

"Well, they must have been thinking about her. I mean, she could have had a lot of influence on state policy. Now that she's dead, her ideas probably won't do as well."

"Good."

"You think she was wrong?"

"I think whoever killed her did God's own work."

I DROVE THE TWENTY-FIVE miles back to our part of Greater Chicagoland in a thoughtful frame of mind. Good old Uncle Ben had more resolution and more power than I had given him credit for.

At one point I said, "You did a solid job of that, Uncle Ben," trying to keep surprise out of my voice. He must have heard some surprise, anyway.

"Well, it *is* what I do, after all."

"I hadn't known you were such a public speaker. I knew you were an *organizer*—"

"You simply never came to a meeting before."

"Not lack of interest, Uncle Ben. Lack of time."

"Hmmmp."

After a few more miles, he said, "This car is a disgrace, Catherine. Why do you have to keep it so sloppy?" There was a small pile of papers on the floor in front of him.

"Those are extra notebooks. Just in case."

"Why do you keep your dirty laundry on the backseat?"

"That's not dirty laundry; that's disguises."

"Catherine, that's not funny."

"No, I'm not trying to be. If I want to look older, I carry that blocky purse—see the white plastic thing?—and wear those high-heeled pumps and the polyester pantsuit and I look ten years older and totally harmless. And if I want to look younger, I use that—well, it's underneath, you can't see it—but I put that stiffening gunk on my hair and wear—you see that stuff that looks like mattress ticking and housedresses?—I put on half a dozen different patterns and make sure the shirt hangs out longer under the jacket and I look ten years younger."

"That's appalling."

"Well, it's not *dishonest!* I still tell people my right name. It's just if you look a little like them, they trust you more."

He thought about that for a couple of miles. Then he laughed. It was a honking laugh, but real. "Say, Catherine—" he said.

"Yes?"

"Could we stop on Dixie Highway for something?"

"Sure. What?"

"There's a ribs place that makes french-fried onion rings."

"Sure," I said, thinking I was pretty tired, but why not? "A special favorite of yours?" There was a lot I didn't know about Uncle Ben.

"Um, yes." He hesitated. "I just love onion rings, and Elise won't allow them in the house."

HE ATE ONION RINGS half of the remaining distance home. He said, "Oh, my, that was good." Then he sighed with satisfaction and lit up a cigar. Between the odor from the onion-rings bag and the cigar, he was fumigating the car. Maybe later tonight the smell would repel auto thieves, but right now it wasn't worth gagging and watering eyes.

"Say, Uncle Ben? Would you mind putting your window down a little?"

The adrenaline of the meeting was now running down, and he was riding along with his head hanging low. He

seemed satisfied with himself, though. He wound down his
window cheerfully enough. Not far enough but cheerfully
enough.

"Where'd Torkel go, Uncle Ben?"

"Home."

"By himself? He just comes out with the flyers and then
goes on home and doesn't want to talk with us or, you
know, have a cup of coffee? An ice cream cone? Fried on-
ions?"

"Torkel is a loner."

"Why is he in PASA, then?"

"Why not? He believes in its goals. A person doesn't have
to be Mr. Sociability to have beliefs and to try to help people who have the same beliefs."

UNCLE BEN LIVED in a high-rise half a block from Lake
Michigan. His building had no view of the lake, which
dropped it out of the stratosphere-rent district, but the lake
breezes plus the possibility of walking to the lake in the
summer had to put the rent in the medium-high range.

When we pulled up in front of his place, Ben said, "I'd
ask you in, Catherine. Your aunt Elise would love to see
you, I'm sure. But she hasn't been feeling well."

"That's okay, Uncle Ben."

"She's probably gone to bed."

"Sure. That's where I'm headed myself."

TWELVE

ONE OF THE PROBLEMS with writing as a way of making a living is that people don't treat it as real work, as a business, with a product that has to be got out. I have friends who will phone me any time of day and ask me to go to the Lincoln Park Zoo with them and a visiting friend. I'll say, "I'm working," and they'll say, "Well, but you're just writing today, aren't you?" Just writing indeed!

Probably they distinguish writing from actually *interviewing* or researching, which may seem more like work. In fact, it's the other way around. Interviewing is relatively easy, except for finding a parking place. Writing is hard.

People who read a finished article in a magazine think all you have to do is get the facts and then "just put them together." Not so. If it seems effortless on paper, it probably cost blood. It's the ones you don't do well that wind up as hard reads. You can't just put all the facts in chronological order, because many happened at the same moment and some are nonchronological, anyway, like descriptions of industrial products or why cholesterol isn't good for you. You need to find a grabber, you need organization, you need a punch line.

And you need nerves of Kevlar to survive when the editor takes the product of blood and says, "Not too bad. Just come up with a different way to handle this."

Besides the fact that your friends may not treat writing as real work, there is the danger that one may, oneself, not treat it as real work. Working at home is no small hump to get over. The day is filled with land mines. It's all too easy to decide to take a nap or bake chocolate chip cookies. Or—

most dangerous of all—to wait for inspiration. Someone said the writer who waits for inspiration is a fool.

Early on it hits you that you either will get next to nothing done or you will be professional—work at least an eight-hour day at least five days a week. When you're really into a project, it goes much higher than that.

So I got up Friday morning and scheduled myself three interviews, minimum, with a possible fourth as time permitted.

Number one. Ten A.M. Charles Jaffee. If he wasn't guilty, maybe he noticed something, and anyway, why did he run out? This interview was strictly business. There was no intent on my part to keep in with a rich, handsome, worldly man who knew how to dress and how to order wine. And if you believe that, I have this really undervalued stock in a silver mine in Nicaragua . . .

Number two. Noon. Glen Barton of the DEA. If Louise Sugarman had got her way, what would happen to people with jobs in the Drug Enforcement Administration?

Number three. Two P.M. Dr. Cameron Lloyd. Other than Robert Erdmann, he was Louise Sugarman's heir apparent.

Number four. Planned, but no appointment made. Aunt Elise Hoskinson. Why? Well, there was more to good old Uncle Ben than I had thought, determinationwise. And I wondered whether she had a hatred of drugs herself and was egging him on. Aunt Elise had always been pleasant, what I had seen of her. But we didn't meet all that often. Would an apparently gentle, middle-aged couple blow up a pleasant white-haired old lady?

Not ordinarily. But drugs seem to do strange things to people, whether they use them or not.

CHARLES JAFFEE'S OFFICES were located just three blocks from Aunt Elise and Uncle Ben's apartment. Three blocks and $30 million.

Jaffee had two of the top floors of a building on the outer rive, overlooking the lake. This is Chicago's Gold Coast. f Chicago is a city of neighborhoods, this is its longest, arrowest neighborhood, one of real money, stretching everal miles, but never more than one building wide. Put nother way, a beach in Chicago is a strip of beautiful light and bordered on one side by water and on the other side by vealth.

Interesting that Jaffee had his office here, though. I had ind of pegged him as the type for the John Hancock Center. The Hancock is on Michigan Avenue, not at all a shabby ddress, either. But the major advantage of the Hancock is nat you can have, say, a suite or a floor of offices seventy r eighty stories above the street. If it's raining in Chicago, n the top floors of the Hancock the sun may be shining, nd you can look down on a bank of clouds.

Talk about being above the masses.

I had an interviewee who lived in an apartment up there. he building was so tall it swayed. She told me that if a trong wind was blowing you could lie in a bath and watch he water slowly slide back and forth. I made an excuse to se her bathroom while I was there and, by jiminy, she was ight. The water in the toilet bowl was sashaying back and orth.

Although technically, I supposed the water was standing till and the rest of the room was moving.

At any rate, Jaffee's building was not trendy Michigan venue but expensive, traditional Lakeshore Drive. Walut-paneled elevator. Doorman who phoned Jaffee's suite, shered me into the elevator, and closed its door. I had the eeling he would have liked to check my Dun & Bradstreet ating. The elevator went to the anteroom of Jaffee's offices and nowhere else. It's odd to get in an elevator and not ush any button at all. It just goes up, and when it stops, ou're where you were going, so to speak.

And himself standing there to greet me! Even his lacquered secretary, seated at a desk the size of a Cadillac, couldn't help showing surprise at his attention to me.

"Catherine! You honor our poor house."

"That would take a lot of doing."

He led the way to a corner office. The oak parquet was highly polished. A dark red and light blue Oriental rug lay in the center. High, arched windows were spaced along the two outside walls, and between them, set diagonally, was Charles's desk, and the desk spoke to me. It said Very Major Antique. The third wall was occupied by floor-to-ceiling glass-fronted oak bookcases. The fourth wall was oak paneled. In front of it was a leather sofa, faced at ninety degrees by two leather chairs. There was no excess here; nothing you could say was there for show, nothing trendy, not even a sculpture, and the only painting, over the sofa, proved to be one of Charles's mother. But, oh, how the room whispered money.

Charles bypassed the desk and led the way to the sofa. I sat. He sat facing me.

"Is this visit social? Unfortunately, the time of day suggests it's business."

"I'm afraid it is." Well, for all I knew, a little playing hard to get made women more attractive to Charlie. Certainly he would have enough who threw themselves at him.

"When Louise Sugarman was killed," I said, "I was not in a position to see everything that was going on."

"That's an understatement. How are you? Are you over the headaches?"

"Mostly. Thanks. I wondered whether, just before the bomb was detonated, you saw anybody holding anything shaped sort of like a penlight?"

"Do you mean an actual penlight? There were people with pens."

"Something cylindrical, at least four inches long, I would think. Pointed toward Lousie—and me." I didn't mention the cigarette-package bomb. McCoo might not want me to.

and anyway, why not keep something back? You never know.

"Um." Charles stared into space.

After a minute he said, "There was that woman from the PTA. The black woman. She had a necklace. Big thing. She kept fingering it."

"Did she point it at us?"

"If she did, I didn't see her do it. But I wasn't watching her especially, right then. The economist had a pen, a fat red pen, as I remember."

"Robert Erdmann?"

"Yes. That very strange young man who follows Ben Hoskinson around—the young man with the blond hair and red face? He had something in his hand."

"Torkel. Did he point it?"

"Not that I know of. Let's see. There were probably several others."

"Uncle Ben?"

"Not that I can remember. Louise Sugarman's husband had a newspaper. You could hide things in a newspaper. What's this about? Are you thinking there was a detonator?"

"Yes, there must have been something or other."

"The bomb couldn't have been on a timer?"

"Well, think of it this way." I was still protecting my source. "If the bomb had just been left there, set to go off in whatever, say, ten minutes, it could have caught anybody. There was no way to know that Louise and I would necessarily sit down. And right at that time."

"You're sure it was intended for her?"

"What! Aren't you? Isn't everybody?"

"I suppose so," he said slowly. "Must have been." He seemed to be thinking about something else.

The door opened. An elderly man in a black suit entered with a tray. Without a word, he placed it on the table in front of us. Charles said, "Thank you, Howard." The man left.

There were demitasse cups on the tray, a steaming carafe, and a plate of tiny croissants, each no more than two inches long. Charles poured and handed me a cup.

"Must have been," he said, again thoughtfully.

"Surely you don't think it was intended for *me?*"

"No, I don't see why. Of course"—he grinned—"I don't know who you've offended lately. You can't write articles without annoying people, I would think."

"That's for sure. Even if you write a complimentary profile of a well-known person, you annoy all his enemies." I munched a croissant. It was perfect—warm, chewy, buttery. More calories, but this was no time to worry. I wouldn't want him to think I didn't appreciate his thoughtfulness. Charles put down his cup and took out that beautiful cigarette case. He held it out to me. I leaned forward to see what brand he smoked. Camel. The odds were, of course, that whoever planted the bomb never smoked Carlton 120's. It would have been stupid for anybody to use his own brand.

I waited for Charles to take a cigarette. I wanted to see how he put it out. It had been galling that I had not watched when we went to La Dolce Pesche, but at that time I had not remembered the mashed *J* shape of the butts in the ashtray.

"The objection would be the same, anyway," he went on, taking back the case. "They wouldn't know you'd sit there, either. It's not impossible, though, that they didn't care *who* they blew up," he said.

"Why?"

"Well, say somebody objected to the whole idea of the conference. The subject matter. Drugs. Say somebody doesn't think a great university should dignify repeal by having a symposium in the first place."

"You're right, I guess. That's not impossible."

"A bomb is a general commentary. What an age we live in."

"I don't believe it, though."

"Oh? Why not?"

I didn't tell him the fact that there really had been a detonator made it nonsense. I respected McCoo's confidence. "They just happen to get the most controversial person at the symposium? That's too much good luck on their part for me to swallow."

"You're probably right."

He closed the case. He wasn't going to smoke. Hell. But then again, he was no longer a suspect.

"Good coffee," I said.

Taking the hint, he reached over and poured me more. He was efficient in his gestures, graceful, really. Didn't spill a drop. The cuff link that showed when he reached forward contained no ostentatious jewels. Just a plain cubic chunk of solid gold.

"And you know," he said lazily, "I think they could have known that Louise Sugarman would sit there."

"Really? How?"

"They wouldn't know who would sit with her, maybe, or who would sit closer to the table. Which is a problem. But they could guess she'd sit down if she could."

"Why? Tell me!"

"She'd had a hip replacement three or four years back. Except when she had to give a speech, she didn't like to be on her feet too long."

When I stood up to go, he came over and stood near me. Without saying a word, he touched my hair. Then he picked it up, held my hair in his hand, and kissed the back of my neck.

I did not need any more romantic complications in my life. John and Mike were complicated enough. But really, could it *hurt* just to get to know Charles a little bit?

By the time I left, I had agreed to see him for dinner three nights later. Did I have a date with Mike? Had I intended to try to patch things up with John? I couldn't quite remember.

Oh, well. Oh, wow.

THIRTEEN

LASALLE STREET IS THE street of lawyers. Just off LaSalle, on Madison, Monroe, and Randolph streets, are the major county, state, and federal buildings. The Daley Building, which houses the Cook County civil courts, is here. So is the Dirksen Federal Building. So is city hall. An attorney can work anywhere in this rectangle and walk to almost every building of importance to him.

The representative the Drug Enforcement Administration had sent to the symposium, Glen Barton, had granted me an interview in his office in the Hekman Building on LaSalle Street. No surprise. It was one of half a dozen buildings in the area named after assorted politicians.

His office was on the third floor.

I remembered the face as soon as I saw him. Smoothly shaven, boyish, but slick, not innocent. Well, of course, the agency would send a person to a symposium who would look well for them. Somebody who could talk, too. Somebody who would not respond hastily to attacks from people who did not agree with him. Somebody impenetrable.

And now in a one-on-one situation, on his own turf, he would probably be even harder to get at. I had a sinking feeling that this would not go well.

"Ms. Marsala?" He held out a well-manicured hand. Smooth light blue shirt, sharply creased dark blue pants. This was the sort of person for whom permanent press was born.

"Mr. Barton. Good of you to see me."

"I'm not quite sure what it is I can do for you. Please sit down."

The setting was institutional. He had done very little to make it his own. There was a photo on his desk. Wife and two children. He was the type to rent a photo if he didn't have a family of his own. No, that was unfair. But he was the type that made me feel like attacking.

"Terrible thing that happened to you," he was saying. "Are you over any ill effects?"

"I am. Louise Sugarman isn't."

"No, of course not."

"What did you think of her, Mr. Barton?"

"Sincere. Well-meaning. I'm sure she didn't have any ax to grind in spite of her pernicious views."

"Pernicious?"

"You know, it is the position of the government of the United States that drugs are capable of destroying the fabric of society."

"Federal agencies, of course, aren't supposed to have views of their own. They're supposed to respond to the will of the people. Isn't that right?"

"Of course."

"By ax to grind, you meant—"

"I said I believed she didn't have an—"

"You meant that a person with her views might have an interest in drug running?"

"I didn't believe it of her. I've already said—"

"But wouldn't a person who wanted to make money on illegal sales be *opposed* to decriminalization?"

"They might go into—"

"Do you think if drugs were decriminalized she could make money from them? Wouldn't the prices fall, and wouldn't any illegal drug peddlers go out of business?"

"Just speaking theoretically, I suppose one would form it into a legal business."

"Now, when you say you're sure she didn't have an ax to grind, are you saying that your organization had investigated her?"

"No, I'm not saying that."

"*Did* you investigate her?"

"We don't give out information on our investigations to reporters."

"So there was an investigation?"

"Nor do we reveal even whether there are any such investigations."

"Not even if a person were to apply under the Freedom of Information Act?"

"Ms. Marsala, there is an exception for situations where governmental investigators might be compromised."

"They would be compromised if you told me which undercover investigators investigated her. They wouldn't be compromised if you simply told me such an investigation took place." My head was starting to ache. He looked as cool and smooth as ever.

"I cannot tell you whether such an investigation took place."

He smiled. Bastard.

"Let me ask a different question, then. If Louise Sugarman had her way, wouldn't you be out of business?"

"What are you asking?"

"If Louise Sugarman had her way and drugs were decriminalized, you'd be out of a job."

"No."

"This is an enormous organization, and it's built entirely on the base of countering the traffic in illegal drugs. If they were legal, that would be the end of this organization."

"No, Ms. Marsala. This organization is federal."

"What does that have to do with it?"

"Ms. Sugarman's proposal was that the state of Illinois get out of the business of enforcing laws against drugs. Somewhat the way Oregon and Alaska have decriminalized marijuana."

"Right."

"But the federal laws against the drug traffic would still be in place. Traffic across state lines would still be a federal crime. And how else would drugs get into Illinois except across state lines? Even if they crossed state lines undetected, federal agents would no doubt still have the right to arrest people in the state of Illinois who had drugs in their possession, under any relevant federal statutes. Just as federal agents can arrest and prosecute people for violating other people's civil rights, even in states that don't have any civil rights statutes themselves."

Oh. Also oh-oh. I did what I always do when faced with an embarrassing response. I whipped out my notepad and one of my many pens and wrote down what he had said. "Federal statutes," I mumbled, to show I was concentrating. The only thing you can do is tough these situations out.

"So you didn't have any reason to blow her up," I said, smiling broadly.

He leaned back in his swivel chair and put his hands behind his head. "Nope."

"Did you like her?"

He swung down fast. "I did not like her. She was playing on people's gullibility. Easy solutions to hard questions. Her ideas, let me say it again, were pernicious."

"Despite what you say, she must have been threatening to you."

"Why?"

"Let's say she succeeded here. So Illinois saves a lot of money in enforcement. And maybe the treatment programs start working pretty well, too. So another couple of states try it. And maybe they don't fall apart, either. Oregon hasn't. The end of the world does *not* come. So another dozen states chime in. The next thing you know, their people in Congress are asking why the feds are spending so much money on the problem if it's not necessary. After a while, maybe they cut back on those federal statutes and then on the funding for the DEA. And then maybe they cut out the DEA entirely. How about *that*?"

He leaned back again.

"With the present climate of opinion in this country, Ms. Marsala—"

"Mmm?"

"You and I will both have white hair and be eating pabulum before that happens."

Stonewalled. Shut out. Defeated. Down for the count.

Not every interview goes well. I don't always get a wonderful quotation or flush out an unguarded remark. But I am always mad at myself when I fail. Hell and damnation! What a zero!

I was out of Mr. Smooth's office before twelve-thirty. There wasn't much point in staying longer. I couldn't budge him, and none of the techniques that worked with more emotional souls—such as just sitting there, waiting for him to blurt out something unguarded—worked with him. He was capable of looking blandly back at me, making a tent out of his fingers, or, equally frustrating, reciting the goals and guidelines of the DEA.

I wouldn't put *anything* past him, but that didn't mean he'd blown up Louise Sugarman. One thing about these federal officials—all of them, state's attorneys, FBI guys, the whole shooting match. They are never locals. They are always imports from other states, and they never stay in any one locale long. This is done intentionally to keep them outsiders. They don't develop ties. They are less susceptible to bribes. The federal agencies have it down to a system exactly how long to leave an agent in one place before they should be moved on.

So I really doubted that Glen Barton, federal agent, could have a personal antipathy to a state personality like Louise.

Then again, what if somebody in the federal government considered her a threat? Now, *that's* an idea! The feds send a hit man. Barton. Much as this sounded like a febrile movie plot, I couldn't entirely discount it. The feds have certainly got up to some funny behavior in recent years.

Zowie, yes. The bee's knees. The real McCoy. The true quill.

GUESSES GET YOU zip in this business.

I had lox and cream cheese on an onion bagel at Hermione's Heaven. Hermione herself was there—isn't she always? She came by the table to tell me I ought to have ordered the sprouts and green pepper salad because I was supposed to be on a diet, wasn't I? But I told her I had been sick and needed the energy, and besides, I had a big afternoon coming up.

So far today I had been walking, as my destinations had all been in the Loop area. This was one of those summer days that September in Chicago gives us. It gives us mighty few, but what there are, are choice. Today was almost too warm.

I hit Dr. Lloyd's office at ten of two for a two o'clock appointment. It's in the college building rather than the med school, because he teaches in both. The door stood wide open. He was sitting behind a cluttered desk, wearing a tweedy brown suit with leather elbow patches and chewing on the end of a pen. We're talking serious professorial typecasting here.

"Oh, Ms. Marsala," he said, looking up. "I'm so glad you're early."

I was amazed at how kindly his eyes were. At the symposium I had only seen him from a distance. He was lovable.

"Dr. Lloyd."

He chewed on his pen while he inclined his head toward a chair for me to sit. Dr. Lloyd taught psychiatry; surely he could tell me what all this chewing on things meant.

"We have a problem," he said, "and I was worried that you might be late. And then I wouldn't know how to reach you—"

He chewed on his lip as he remembered how worried he had been. "The problem is, I've got to leave here in ten minutes."

"Oh?"

"Common Sense has called a meeting. An extraordinary session. An area PTA group in Illinois is going to be debating— Well, see, they want to get out a position paper on students and drug use. So over the next two weeks, they plan to hold local debates. They really intend to have all points of view represented, you see; I think they're quite sincere about that. We've realized that for Common Sense to go any longer without a chairperson is, uh, is an act of folly. I mean, we need a leader. So we called a session for this afternoon at two-thirty."

"Oh."

"And I want to walk because, um, because people ought to walk whenever they can."

"Yes, they should."

"So, you see—"

"Well, I could walk you over—"

"You see, I thought you might as well just come along to the meeting."

"Oh, sure!"

ON THE WALK OVER, chewing on a pencil eraser, he told me how upset he was the day of the symposium to see that I was injured. The death of Louise Sugarman was terrible enough, he said. But she knew the risks. There was a lot of hatred directed toward the repeal people, he said in his gentle voice. I was "an innocent bystander." He hoped I would realize that he had wanted to write to me to sympathize, but since I didn't know him, he felt it would be more of an imposition than a consolation.

The funny thing was, vague as he seemed, I believed he really meant it. He really appeared to care.

"Dr. Lloyd," I said, "why do you chew on pens and paper and things?"

"Oh...Because otherwise I bite my fingernails, and then they look terrible."

"I WANT TO CARRY ON her work as if she had never left us," Max Sugarman said to the audience in conclusion. There were twenty-five or thirty people on the folding chairs in the main room at Common Sense. They were listening politely. Max was making a plea that he be appointed chairperson of the group. But the vibes to me were that the audience was thinking of him as the opening act, not a serious contender.

They applauded lightly. He sat down.

"Should I be here?" I asked Mandy, who happened to have sat next to me.

"Sure. We don't have anything to hide."

"No, I mean, isn't this an in-house sort of thing? Aren't you going to vote on who you want for chair?"

"The board members will vote. But as far as you being here, that's fine. The whole idea is for people to ask questions. Challenge the candidates. The harder the questions, the better. We want to know how they field questions."

"But nobody asked Max Sugarman any questions."

She smiled gently at me.

Cameron Lloyd and Robert Erdmann were the two candidates who mattered. Both sat in front. I heard Lloyd say to Erdmann, "Go ahead."

Erdmann said, "After you."

Cameron Lloyd got up. I thought, No, you fool; the one who goes last has the advantage. But Lloyd, with his nice-guy stroll, was at the lectern.

He smiled at the group. "I would like to take the terror out of drugs so we can fight the effects sensibly," he said. "Nobody forces anybody to take drugs. But our fear of the drugs themselves has become so great that we've passed laws that are hurting us. It's a classic case of the cure that's worse than the disease.

"We need to go on with Louise's campaign, which is essentially to say that we can handle the drug threat without all the fear and crime and death. We should go to the PTA meetings and everywhere else with the message that addiction—any addiction—is a medical problem, not a criminal problem.

"We want people to begin to realize the human cost of our drug laws. Not the financial cost but the cost in conflict between people, between generations, between police and the public, and the cost in human misery.

"We have to make people see that when you make a substance illegal you make it attractive to the very people we want most to protect. Children and young people, particularly adolescents.

"Adolescent risk-taking behavior has always been with us. But when you outlaw something, you put it in the category of forbidden fruit. And suddenly it becomes attractive out of all proportion to any pleasure it can give. Suddenly it's interesting. It's exciting. It's daring. It becomes 'cool' or 'hip' to experiment with it. The words change, but the behavior is always with us.

"Adolescents who are healthy go through a process of exploring the world and asserting their independence. This is natural. They may drive too fast or smoke cigarettes or stay out late at night or experiment with sex. What we've done with our drug laws is put drugs into the category of things they have to try."

A man in front waved his arm. "But Dr. Lloyd! They try the other things, anyway. Cigarettes and alcohol, for instance."

"Both cigarettes and alcohol are considered 'adult' by adolescents because they are sold only to adults. It's illegal for adolescents to buy them. Drugs are even more exciting because they're illegal. But we turn a problem into a tragedy when a teenager caught with drugs may have criminal penalties imposed on him. If he has sold drugs to friends, he may wind up in a state or federal prison, where he will probably be sexually abused and certainly will be exposed to criminal ways of thinking and acting. And he will have a lifelong police record.

"The saddest thing is, if we can simply get young people through this adolescent phase, they mature; they don't turn back to risk-taking behavior, by and large. All of this behavior is concentrated in the years between twelve and the early twenties."

Mandy asked, "Is this true about everyone?"

"Pretty nearly. There are biological factors that regulate this. It has nothing to do with criminality or being 'bad boys' or 'bad girls.' A substance called monoamine oxadase, which regulates the level of some brain chemicals like serotonin, is negatively correlated with risk-taking behavior. The lower the MAO, the more risk taking. Not only do adolescents with the lowest MAO have the most risk-taking behavior, but the levels of MAO start to rise about the age of twenty-two. Biological maturity sets in. This is normal. What I'm saying is that we need as a culture, as a society, to understand the development young people go through. We need to *handle* their risk-taking stage and manage it without giving them criminal consequences for normal behavior."

A person out of my line of sight shouted, "You don't win a war by giving up. This isn't going to win the war on drugs."

"But what do we mean by war?" Lloyd asked, smiling. "If we wage a war on tooth decay, and we have done just that in this country, we do it with education and medical tools, not with armed forces. You treat a medical problem with medical armaments."

I figured I'd get in the act: "Is that what's happening with alcoholism?"

"In the sense that we're just beginning to recognize that alcoholism is a disease and that in many or most cases it's genetic. And therefore we're starting to treat it rather than throw people in jail for being drunks. But adolescent risk-taking is *not* a disease. It's a perfectly normal stage of development, like nest-making behavior is at the height of the reproductive years. It's time we grew up as a society and stopped being terrified of it.''

"You going to want cocaine sold in every grocery store? What's to stop twelve-year-olds from getting it, then?'' said another voice.

"Deglamorization.''

"What?''

"During Prohibition alcohol consumption *increased*. Increased! A psychologist could have predicted this. Because suddenly it became glamorous. It was exciting to have a bootlegger. It was risky and romantic to go to speakeasies. That's what we're doing with kids and drugs today.''

An older woman stood up. I suspected she was one of the board. She had board member written all over her sturdy face. "All right,'' she said, "but even so, some of them are going to try it. It may be deglamorized, but it will still be something to experiment with. You make it available, they'll be standing around stoned on every street corner.''

"Colleges today ask incoming freshmen whether they smoke cigarettes and whether they want to room with people who smoke. Ninety percent answer no to both questions. Cigarette smoking is *way* down among adolescents. It's been deglamorized. Now it's considered unhealthy, unpleasant, stupid, and it gives you bad breath.''

"Oh, but that's just cigarettes—''

"Cigarette smoking is a harder habit to break than alcoholism or heroin addiction. And much harder than marijuana, which is pretty trivial. Marijuana, in fact, tends to be tried and then dropped. One-third of the people who try it enjoy it. One-third try it and find it distasteful. One-third try it and find it has no effect whatsoever. People just give it up after a while. Heroin? Very few people want to stick needles in their veins just for fun. Cocaine is the most attractive, but not very dangerous to health unless it's mixed with something hazardous. And as a habit it's relatively easily broken, too. Easier than most prescription tranquilizers. Kids have given up cigarettes because cigarettes have been deglamorized and the health dangers have been well publicized.

"Alcohol consumption on college campuses is down, too.

"The program we need is: First, get drugs out of the criminal punishment system. Do away with violence and pushers. Two, deglamorize drugs. Three—like cigarettes—publicize health risks. And four, for those kids who have a real psychological problem or a home situation so bad that any sort of mind-deadening drug seems better than reality, don't treat the symptom, *treat the problem*.

"If we're going first of all to the PTAs, we have to have a message that is tailored to the group they're worried about—students. Especially the child between twelve and twenty-one. The present laws aren't working, and they're sending children to prison. We need a consistent, *sane* program. We've had enough hysteria."

A lot of applause. I'd liked his manner and his approach. He was as low-key as Louise had been. If you ask me, and of course nobody would, the Cameron Lloyd manner was the ideal one for the message. He was non-threatening, gentle, commonsensical.

The emcee said, "Our last speaker, Professor Robert Erdmann."

FOURTEEN

ROBERT ERDMANN LOOKED like the "after" picture in one of those self-help books, the kind that teach you how not to be nervous while facing a crowd and engaging in public speaking. I mean, we're talking industrial-strength self-confidence here. Whereas Lloyd was deferential, even when he was giving technical information, Erdmann looked as if we were now going to hear from the Mount.

"Thank you, Cam," he said toward Lloyd. "I agree with you. We have to emphasize the children. *But not exclusively.* In the next weeks we'll be talking with PTA groups, but in the next year we will be talking with everybody. And our attention has to be on the broad picture. The total *cost* of criminalizing drugs.

"The bill for drugs in this country, *just for the drugs alone,* is in excess of eighty billion dollars. That's what the stuff sells for on the open market. And believe me, the market is open. What the stuff would be worth without the inflated prices caused by criminalization is a tiny fraction of that amount, perhaps five billion. Ninety-five percent of the selling price is *caused* by the laws.

"In addition to the eighty-plus billion spent for the drugs themselves, at least twenty billion is spent to *fight* drugs.

"In other words, in excess of a hundred and ten billion dollars in this country is being thrown out the window.

"The country simply cannot afford this kind of hemorrhage.

"There are more costs. People estimate that close to fifty percent of all property crime in the United States is committed by drug users to get money for drugs. These people are wrong! In private, law-enforcement personnel will tell you the figure is much higher. Probably eighty to ninety percent of all muggings are drug related. And what about murder? A Chicago state's attorney prosecuting a drug-related felony murder recently said that in his career he has rarely seen a murder that was not in some way drug connected.

"Our position, the position of Common Sense, is not weird or oddball or unrealistic. It is the future. In 1987, a committee on law reform of the New York County Lawyer's Association recommended that cocaine and heroin be decriminalized. Among other things, they point out that there is no relation between the dangerousness of a drug to the user and the punishment meted out for it. Both alcohol and cigarettes are more dangerous to your health than marijuana. In fact, as I have often said, if you wanted to keep people from doing things that were bad for them, everyone who was more than a hundred percent over his best weight should be arrested and put in prison with limited food."

The firm-faced woman said, "You're not taking into account heroin fatalities—"

"I'm getting to that," he said crisply, dismissing her. "We also have to realize that virtually *all* the deaths from heroin use are not from the heroin itself at all. They are from contaminated needles, or other substances used to dilute the drug. Or from accidental overdose, where the drug the user has bought is not as diluted as he is accustomed to, so he takes more than he thinks he is taking. These are effects not of the drug but of criminalization. Virtually *all* the heroin deaths would disappear with legalization."

"But the numbers of users would increase," I said, just to be provocative.

"Wrong. Heroin, oddly enough, is a drug whose use has *not* increased. The percentage of people using it has stayed about the same since 1915. To most people, it is just not very attractive.

"Now let's talk about other costs for a minute. Prisons, for example. The drug bill in 1987 created thousands of new narcotics officers. Somebody has to pay for them. The penalties for drug possession and sales were increased. Thousands upon thousands of additional people were arrested. They were sentenced to longer prison terms. Somebody has to pay for that. More prisoners are serving longer terms, so now the justice department is talking about needing to double the capacity of federal prisons. Somebody has to pay for that, too.

"The commission said that in 1970, seventeen percent of the federal prisoners were there on drug charges. In 1980 it was twenty-five percent. In 1987, thirty-seven percent. The 1990 estimate is almost fifty percent. This is the result of the present drug laws.

"Inside the prisons the situation is increasingly dangerous. The more crowding, the more volatility, the more potential for violence, the more prison deaths. Here in Illinois, Governor Thompson's Determinate Sentencing Act is putting people in prison for longer sentences. A director of one of Illinois' watchdog organzations said we would need a new 750-bed prison every year for ten years to keep up with the demand, and there isn't the money available for it.

"Meanwhile, while we're bleeding to death paying for prisons, you've got a thousand serious toxic waste sites in Illinois and no money to clean them up. Radioactive pollution, leaking underground gasoline tanks where the gas is seeping into the well water, heavy metals, and PCBs in the soil. We can't repair our streets because there's no money. We can't maintain the quality of our grade schools without massive increases in property taxes. Cities are strangling on costs, and basic services aren't getting done.

"And at the same time, you've got people spending money on absolutely asinine drug programs. In Indiana this year, they had state troopers running around four counties destroying wild marijuana plants. The joyful news was in the papers—twenty-three million wild plants destroyed. Besides, they distributed weed killer to farmers to help them destroy more plants. Can you imagine the expense and the time involved? Somebody had to pay for that. Plus—these are troopers who could have been arresting drunk drivers before they killed somebody or patrolling streets for muggers. The marijuana plants, by the way, were planted in Indiana and Michigan during World War I for hemp to be used for rope. And the dumbest thing of all—they eradicate these things every year, and surprise! The next year they spring right back up again.

"Just like the drug problem.

"Oregon has decriminalized marijuana. In Alaska you can even grow it in your yard without getting into trouble. And neither state has sunk into anarchy.

"At the same time, in Wisconsin, stiffer penalties for drugs are making their way through the state legislature. Selling five and a half pounds of marijuana?—ten years in prison and a hundred-thousand-dollar fine. Ten grams of heroin (which is a third of an ounce, less than a tablespoon)—fifteen years in prison and a five-hundred-thousand-dollar fine!

"A heroin habit is now costing a user about a hundred dollars a day. Cocaine more. People mug and kill for that kind of money. In New York City there are about two hundred thousand intravenous drug users. Sophisticated studies suggest that at least half of those would turn themselves in for treatment if there was treatment available and if they weren't penalized criminally when they showed their faces. Thus taking a hundred thousand potential muggers off the streets! In the Netherlands, seventy percent of the drug users are in methadone maintenance programs or treatment programs. But private and public agencies *together* in New York can handle about thirty thousand. Take the two hundred thousand IV users and add another two hundred thousand others who use cocaine or designer drugs and thirty thousand treatment slots is seven percent. Which is not a solution.

"We are hurling more laws and harsher penalties at a medical problem, and it isn't working.

"And it isn't economical. Bottom line. An addict who is mugging for a hundred dollars a day is taking $36,500 a year from people, let alone the pain and fear and humiliation of the people who are mugged. A methadone maintenance program costs *under a thousand dollars* a year.

"I'll give you an Illinois cost sheet, and then I'll end this. Illinois spends sixty million dollars on substance-abuse programs a year. Two hundred and sixty million on children and family services. And probably half of that is for families who can't make it because of somebody's expensive drug habit. The department of corrections?—$413 million. At *least* half of that is drug punishment. Mental health?—seven hundred million. I'll leave it to you to guess how much of that is drug related. Public aid three and a half billion. *Billion*. Public health about a hundred and eighty million. The state police a hundred and fifty million.

"These figures don't include county governments or city and town governments. Municipal police. Local jails.

"One of the presidential hopefuls suggested during his campaign that we apportion a billion dollars more for the Coast Guard to keep drugs out of this country. A billion dollars! Think of the treatment centers we could set up with that kind of money! But what he didn't realize is that even if it were spent it would be money down a rat hole. Build a Great Wall of China all around the nation, bomb the countries that raise coca and opium, and the *only change* would be that basement labs would spring up all over the country to make synthetic cocaine. It is already chemically possible. When it's lucrative enough, it will be done. And then we will start having deaths from cocaine use, because not everybody will manufacture the stuff right, and some of it will be deadly.

"A billion dollars!

"Billions of dollars that we don't have. That we need for other problems, like education. Wasted police time that could be spent on real crime. Police corrupted because of the colossal amount of money involved.

"Billions and billions of dollars into the hands of organized crime, *just because* this stuff is illegal. And enormous pressure on weak little people with sad little habits to
start selling, to encourage friends and children to become
users, to help pay for their own habits.

"A habit that would cost pennies if the stuff were decriminalized.

"If even a fraction of those billions were put into treatment programs, every addict in the state could have clean,
safe maintenance medication or counseling, and there would
still be billions of dollars saved.

"And the saving in human health would be enormous."

WELL, ERDMANN BLEW them away. You could just look
around the room and see that. It was written on their faces.
Erdmann would go out into the world and have the facts and
figures and *no*body was going to shout him down or look at
him as if he were a poor little thing with an oddball point of
view.

Personally, I liked Lloyd better. Erdmann was hard and
aggressive, while Lloyd was softer. He accepted questions
as if they were sincere and well meant, not the product of an
idiot brain obscured by nasty intentions. Lloyd either really
sympathized with people or did an awfully good job of
looking as if he did.

On television, Lloyd would be one of those people who
are likable. Not Erdmann.

But if the board didn't pick Erdmann, I'd eat my Bic.

The room buzzed with postdebate debate. Mandy took
charge of me.

"Help me get the beverages?" she asked.

In the alcove at the top of the stairs were Styrofoam cups.
On the stairs were piled six-packs of Coke. Coca Cola, not
coke, you understand. There were two six-packs, one piled
on the other, all the way down, at the extreme left of every
stair. You wouldn't trip on them if you paid attention to
where you were going. Mandy saw me looking in surprise.

"Well, we just don't have any storage space," she said.

I carried out two six-packs and the tower of Styrofoam cups. Mandy took four six-packs and lugged them up. By the time we got to the table in the main room, Rufe was coming in the front door with a big bag of ice.

This collected the crowd.

Mandy almost whispered to me: "The board members are voting in the back room."

"Oh." Erdmann came strolling confidently past. "Want a Coke, Professor Erdmann?" I asked. He smiled.

"Sure."

Lloyd came up and poured his own.

People fired questions at them both. I heard Erdmann say, as he turned away from me toward a group of men, "Did you know the Inter-American Affairs Bureau in the State Department proposed that we pay two thousand dollars to every Bolivian farmer who agreed to plant any crop other than coca, the source of cocaine?"

"When you say proposed," said a deep manly voice—the kind that makes his every remark sound important—"may I take it that the proposal fell through?"

"Not exactly. The proposal drew a lot of flak. Another agency called it immoral."

"I should think so! What a costly precedent it would set! Countries could hold us up for ransom—"

"*But,*" said Erdmann, riding firmly over these remarks, "instead, the United States upped its aid to Bolivia and handed the Bolivians the responsibility for doling out the money as subsidies."

"I wonder how much of that ever really was distributed?"

"But the point is," Erdmann finished, "for every two thousand dollars to a Bolivian farmer, you could keep two addicts in a methadone program for a year!"

I was pouring Coke with one hand, shifting cups with another, and asking myself silently whether Erdmann would

ill for a position in the limelight with lots of opportunity
o debate.

Does Michael Jackson dance?

Would a Chicago councilman take a bribe?

As a murderer, to me, Cameron Lloyd was far less likely.
And for that matter, his ability to take over Common Sense
must have always been less likely than for Erdmann to do it.
So—back burner Cameron Lloyd, as least tentatively. As for
Max Sugarman, of course, he was really out of the running. I guessed that at the present moment the probability
of each candidate's being given Louise Sugarman's mantle
was something like this:

Robert Erdmann 85 percent Cameron Lloyd 15 percent Max Sugarman 0 percent

I would bet the likelihood of each being the killer was very
similar.

Just then a voice said, "Ms. Marsala!" Max Sugarman
stood smiling behind me.

"Hello. Quite a turnout."

"Yes, it's very gratifying. Shall we get some soft drinks
for everyone?"

"They're right here," I said, pointing to the table in front
of us.

"Oh, so they are. How efficient you all are! How did you
think my talk went?"

"Uh, very nicely."

"I'm sorry about Bob and Cam, though."

"How do you mean?"

"Well, they would have been fine, too, but—"

"But?"

"I'm sure the committee will give it to me. What with my
relationship with Louise, and knowing her programs, and
then I could see people just really warming up to me as I
spoke—"

My head started making *Twilight Zone* music, and cold fingers crept up my spine.

This was big-league, major loss of the sense of reality.

FIFTEEN

'M NOT PROUD OF what I did next. I ran out. Me, who usually wants so badly to hang tough. If there's any excuse, maybe the concussion wasn't entirely gone and I was still suffering some degree of what my fuzzy-cheeked doctor called "emotional lability."

I put down the empty can of Coke I had apportioned between two Styrofoam cups. I smiled stiffly to Max Sugarman and said, "Good luck," and I walked to the door.

Out the door. Walked down the street. Ran down the next block. Ran until I got a pain in my side, then slowed to a walk. My car was at my apartment, anyway, not here, but that was okay, because Mike's office wasn't far. It was now four o'clock. With any luck, he'd be there, typing.

There was some luck, and he was. Little did I know that would be my day's allowance of luck.

Half a glance at me and Mike said, "What's the matter with you?"

He grabbed me and sat me down in a chair, then went out in the hall and came back with a cup of coffee. I swallowed and choked. The coffee was burning hot.

My face probably turned red, because he said, "There. You look better. What hit you?"

"I'm supposed to be at my Uncle Ben's."

"Well, call him. You obviously can't go anywhere right now."

"No, he's not expecting me. That's just the schedule I made for myself for today."

"Aha!" Mike sat.

"You know I don't like being 'Ahaed!' at."

"Neither does anybody. Sometimes we deserve it. Did you overschedule your day?"

"No, I scheduled it."

"And where have you just come from that scared you so much?"

"I am not scared. I'm—I'm—"

"Go ahead. As a professional wordsmith, you ought to be able to think of the word."

"Disoriented."

"Mmm. Okay. Why?"

"For *starters,* I went into this whole project thinking, sure, drugs are evil; they should be illegal. I mean, it was a *given.* Now I'm not so sure. My head's getting spun around."

"Surely you aren't being disoriented by a theoretical discussion—"

"No. Beyond starters, I'm seeing the effect this whole war is having on people. I'm realizing I had some of these feelings all along. About—you know—"

"Ted?"

"Yeah, Teddy." I thought about him for a moment, but it was too sad.

"Besides," I said, "this project has bifurcated itself. I started out working on a Louise Sugarman profile. Then it turned into an investigation of her murder—"

"Nothing wrong with that, basically. Practically every writing project changes between conception and product."

"I know that. But then it spun off an idea for another article on the repeal arguments. I thought of formating it like a debate, one column for pro, one for anti—"

"I don't like that form. I don't think people read it."

"I agree. But now I'm looking for a human-interest approach, some sort of grabber. So I don't even know any more which is my current project and which is my in-the-wings project—"

"What's wrong with that? You get two articles!"

"I don't want two articles! I mean, not first of all. Dammit, Mike! First of all I want whoever blew her up to be *punished!*"

"Okay, okay. Mellow out here." He put his arm around me.

"All of a sudden, the world looks different. I'm seeing well-meaning, intelligent people, and suddenly they look like potential murderers to me. Not only murderers but particularly cowardly murderers. Like they'd blow up a little old lady either because they didn't like her politics or because they want her job or because in the long run she might cost them money."

"Well, of *course.* Murders for reasons like that happen every day."

"But these are *nice people!*"

He sighed. "Here. It's cooled off. Drink some more."

"YOU KNOW WHAT the problem is—" he said about ten minutes later, when he could see my mental balance was improving.

"What?"

"Most of the pieces you do aren't on murder—"

"That isn't true. I did—"

"I said most. I know you've done a few."

"A few!"

"Well, several, then. But not *most.* And the point is, anyway, the ones you've done fall into two categories. There are the cases where somebody has been accused of murder and you think he didn't do it. And you've made a very good case for it, too, by the way. Or there are the cases where the guy did it but he's such a loser, such a sad sack, or so nuts or subnormal that the story really is, 'Why didn't the system find a way to help this character earlier?'"

"So?"

"So here's a case where everybody who could be involved is pretty much educated, intelligent, and what the psychologists call 'under good impulse control.' So you get into it, and naturally they seem like nice people.''

''I am not that naive.''

''I'm not finished. They seem like nice people who plan ahead and don't do dumb things. So suddenly you're faced with somebody out there who has planned very carefully and done something intelligent, in the sense that this act is reasonably likely to get him what he wants, whatever that may be. And you find that very frightening.''

''I don't know,'' I said grudgingly. ''Maybe you're right.''

''Don't get huffy. I find it frightening myself.''

''Oh.''

That was consoling, in its way.

I said, ''You don't think I ought to give it up, then?''

''No. Whoever it is nearly blasted you, too. I'd be mad as hops if it were me. Were you even *thinking* of giving it up?''

''No.'' I smiled at last. ''But I was curious what you'd say.''

''Sneaky.''

''Ah, come on, Mike. You've made me feel better. Which I'm sure is what you wanted to do. Let's go out and eat something with a sinfully large number of calories.''

''Oh, hell, Cat—''

Suddenly I noticed his suitcase in the corner.

''Gee,'' I said. ''What a shame. This time I sort of—need you.''

''Oh, shit. I'd better stay.''

''Well, okay—''

''I can't, though. The piece is going to be typeset Monday.''

A moment's pause.

''Then you have to go,'' I said.

''You would, too, if you had a deadline. Go. Wouldn't you?''

''Absolutely.'' I nodded firmly. ''Where are you going?''

''Back to the Mississippi River. I'm taking Henry Lee Chin, number-two photographer, with me.''

"Where's number one?"

"Fritz? In the sewers. He's photographing the Deep Tunnel Project before the rains come and fill it up so he can't. Chin and I are taking a Rock Island Line train west at five twenty-seven. Oh, hell, Cat, I'm sorry."

"That's okay, Mike."

"Damn."

"Anyway," I said, standing up, "I know of an interview I should have done long before this. I've been putting it off, I guess."

"Take care of yourself, Cat."

"Have fun. Call me when you get back."

"Right. Don't take any wooden rhetoric."

"Yeah. And you. Don't lead with your Chin."

LT. STAN GOTCHKA has what the Chicago Police Department thinks of as a private office. His desk is in a corner of the room and is glassed in, up to about the five-foot mark.

A little sign under his name said Drug Task Force.

Stan was smiling and courteous when I walked in. But there were lines around his eyes I didn't remember, and the vertical lines on his forehead were a label reading Headache in Here. Other officers, some uniformed and some not, came in and out with papers while we talked. "This war on drugs," I asked him, "are you winning it?"

"In a way." He smiled. Stan was big, and he had a big smile. "You can't expect the traffic in drugs to stop. What you do is keep on top of it."

A plainclothes cop entered with a stack of papers for Stan's signature. As Stan signed, I noticed the top cop watching him.

"Goin' okay?" the cop asked as Stan finished.

"Real good!" Stan said enthusiastically. "How about you?"

"Not bad." The man watched Stan doubtfully a half beat longer, then left.

I knew Stan was lying, too, just from body language. But I couldn't think of any neat, clever way of asking what was wrong. Stan and I are long-term acquaintances, but we've never been really close. If Mr. Plainclothes, who obviously worked with Stan all the time, couldn't get an honest answer, how could I?

It was ten after five.

"You get off at five-thirty, Stan?"

"Making a joke, huh, Cat?"

"Well, for all I know, you've been here since six A.M."

"That's pretty damn close."

"So I was thinking of buying you dinner."

"You were, were you? Bribing a Chicago policeman. That's a Class B felony. Or is it Class C? I forget."

Another plainclothes cop came in. This was a woman.

"You wanted these Xeroxes."

Stan said, "Thanks."

She, too, looked at Stan a little too long and then left.

His phone rang. He picked it up, said, "Gotchka."

His face cheered up. Then it drooped.

"All right," he said. "You just do that."

Silence.

"You just go right ahead. Take your time! Take your stuff with you!"

Another silence. Out in the larger room I saw the first cop standing about twenty feet from Gotchka's door, listening. The rest of the room out there had gotten quieter.

"Yeah, you do that! No, not for hours! You just go right ahead!"

I sat very still, looking interestedly at the radiator.

"Anything, anytime. Yeah! Only just don't expect *me* to be there when you do!"

Stan slammed the phone down hard. It cracked.

There was silence in the outer room.

Stan sat there with his face red and his hands clenched. After half a minute he took a deep breath.

"You wanna take me to dinner, Cat?"

"Yes."

"Well, hell, you got yourself a date."

MABEL'S WAS AN institution. It was one of those places with peanut shells on the floor, but it wasn't cute. The place was near enough to the Chicago PD to have a raft of cops but also not far from where some of the transit workers get off work. It was jammed. Big metal bowls of peanuts in the shell were on every table and all down the long zinc bar. Some of the patrons drop the shells neatly on the floor. Some throw them over their shoulders as if they were making a good-luck wish with salt. Some place them neatly on a folded index finger, cock their thumb, and shoot them off like we used to shoot marbles. I mean, at Mabel's it rains and pours peanut shells.

"Hey, Stan. Didn't the health department have something nasty to say about shells all over the floors of bars? About a year or two ago?"

"Yeah."

"Well?"

"Unearthing a scandal, Cat?"

"No. Why?"

"This bar is owned by the sister of a city council member. When the health department comes in here, they don't *see* any peanut shells."

According to Stan, the specialty here was Old Style beer, but if you insisted, you could also get the second specialty, Mabel's Reuben Sandwich. I ordered one of each for each of us. One Old Style, one Reuben.

The sandwiches were big, the way I like them, and cheesy, the way I like them, with extra sauerkraut, the way I like them. "Hey! This place isn't half bad," I said, keeping my eye on Stan's mood.

"You bet. Told you so."

He looked at his sandwich but poured half his beer straight down his throat.

His voice was firm and cheery, and his face looked tragic.

Oh, wow. This was a genuine grade-A reporter-type moral dilemma. You get a person in this kind of mood and they'll sometimes say more than they mean to. But I don't like to take advantage. When you're somebody's shoulder to cry on, they don't stop to think the shoulder's attached to the hand that writes the exposé.

I was not going to use Stan's words against him. Unless he let slip that he was the one who blew up Louise Sugarman (and me, almost). Then he deserved what he got.

"Let's have another beer," he said.

"That one gone already?"

"Cat, this is one beer. I'm a big boy."

"That's for sure. Okay."

One thing I would not do—and many a reporter has done—is *ply* him with beer. But I wasn't going to fight him over it, either.

By eight P.M. we were at a place ten blocks farther west. It was shabbier. In fact, you could call it a dive. But this one, according to Stan, had real English ale and Foster's Lager, which is Australian.

"You gonna mix the ale with beer, Stan?"

"Oh, hell, yes. It's not really mixing. Ale is just beer that never grew up."

"Stan, about this war on drugs. Are you guys winning?"

"Well, see, we're not going to win, exactly."

"What, then?"

"We're sort of running in place. I mean, we're running, and if it's in place and not losing ground, we're doing real good."

"Oh."

Stan put out his cigarette. He smoked it into a tiny nub, then stabbed it straight down in the ashtray until it mushroomed out. Not a flattened *J*.

"Want another Guinness?"

"No, but I'll have a beer."

"My buy. Ale for me, beer for you."

While he was up at the bar, I poured the last inch of my ale into the spittoon.

By ten, we were at Angelo's, about half a dozen blocks north.

"Angelo's has more kinds of beer on draft," he said, "than any other place in Chicago."

"That's gotta be an accomplishment. Chicago bars being like they are."

"You bet."

"And you're an expert."

"Hell, yes."

He had draft Hacker-Pschorr. I had Paulaner Hefe-Weizen. I was getting so I couldn't finish mine. The headache was coming back, plus a kind of pulsing dizziness. When Stan got up for his round, I said,

"Not for me. I'm going to drink this one slowly."

But he came back with a Pilsner Urquell and a Dortmunder Dab. At least that's what it sounded like he said. His speech was getting a little slurry now.

"Stan, I am *not* going to match you beer for beer."

"Why not?"

"It wouldn't be fair."

"Sure it would. Beer for beer."

"Stan, you're bigger than I am. You've got a foot and a half on me in height."

"So we'll take—um—a little off the top." He poured a bit of mine into his.

"That isn't the way it works. You weigh what? Two fifty?"

"Yeahhh." By the way he said it, I knew he weighed a little more.

"I weigh one twenty-five. That means you have twice the body size and probably twice the blood volume, and that means two beers for you *equals* one beer for me."

"Oh! Yeah, sure, Cat. That makes sense."

"Good."

"You're sure easy to get along with, Cat."

"Sure."

"I wish my wife were as easy to get along with as you."

"Oh?"

"She left me, y'know."

"I figured something had happened."

"Moved out." His eyes looked damp. "With a guy."

"That's rough, Stan."

"Yeah."

"Think about something else."

"Sure, Cat. What?"

"Tell me what you thought of Louise Sugarman."

My big question. Tricky the way I led up to it, too. Plus hit a guy when he's down.

Stan said, "Who?"

AT MIDNIGHT WE were in some godawful spot with a go-go dancer. She looked about fourteen and was overweight. In places. But at least this particular dive had hamburgers and fries. I needed food. Stan wouldn't eat.

"I'll have mm-beer," he said.

"Stan, how long have you and your wife been having problems?"

"Oh, 'bout sixteen years."

"No, really, how long?"

"Thassabout it. Las' three months been the worst, I guess. C'n you believe—she says I'm never home."

"Are you home?"

"Nah."

"Well, then."

"Point is, she knew goin' in."

"Stan, about this war on drugs. How's it going?"

"Real crappy. Real crappy."

I had a cup of coffee in front of me that was still half full. I gave him a sip of it, which he drank before he realized it wasn't beer.

"*Yoh!*" He pushed it away. Then he looked straight at me. His eyes were filling up with tears.

"Cat. You know what I wish?"

"What?"

"I wish—I wish ever'body was honest again. Thas what I wish. I wish there wasn' all this dirty money."

"Don't cry, Stan."

"I got frenns who've been cops ten years, twenny years. They don' make much. They got kids in school, kids in college, some guy offers 'em thousands, *thousands,* you know, now's a guy like that gonna say no to a guy like that and money like that? I mean, like that. I mean, it ain' fair, Cat. It ain' fair!"

He was crying on my shoulder. And the next thing I noticed, the dancer was done, the music was off, and everybody in the place was looking at us.

"It ain' *fair!*" he wailed.

A very large man in a white apron that had brown stains on it came over.

"What're you doin' to him, lady?"

"I'm not doing anything to him."

"Ain' fair, Cat!" Stan wailed.

"What're you doin' to him, lady?"

"Holding him up. What's it look like?"

"Well, you can't do it here."

My head ached. My stomach didn't feel good, either. Now my shoulder ached, too. Unobtrusively, I pulled Stan's cop ID out of his pocket. Flashed it fast, as if it were mine.

"Listen, Charlie," I said. "You want us out of here, you call me a cab, and you get somebody to help me carry him. And the faster you do it, the faster you'll be rid of us. But I want that cab out front before we're out that door or you're in deep shit. I know about your dancer."

The shot in the dark, or something, worked. The cab came. The turkey in the apron personally helped us in. Stan said, "It ain' fair."

In the cab he started to cry again.

"Know what I wish?"

"What, Stan?" I said, trying to find his wallet in his pocket. I don't know his address and wouldn't trust him to tell me accurately now.

"I wish—" said Stan.

"Where to, missus?" said the driver, who was from somewhere in the eastern Mediterranean.

"I'm working on it. Just drive around."

"I—what I'd like—what I'd like—what I'd like—" Stan said.

"Got it." An address just off north Milwaukee Avenue. The old Polish district. I stuck the wallet back firmly in Stan's pants pocket, which appeared to give him a jolt enough to get the needle out of the groove.

"What I'd like is for a while I'd arrest burglars!"

"Yeah, Stan."

"Or rapists! Yeah! Or somebody drives drunk, hit-run—that's what I'd like to arrest. Somebody who really hurts people!"

"Yeah, Stan."

"I'd like to arrest murderers and like that."

THE CABBIE AND I found Stan's key. We got in the house. Stan's wife had left, that's for sure, and she hadn't stopped to clean up. We put him on the bed—the bare mattress, actually. I took off his shoes. The cabbie said taking off shoes was not his job. I found a blanket in the closet the wife must have missed and put it over him.

We proceeded back downtown, where I paid the cabbie when he dropped me in front of my apartment.

I ached head to foot. The four steps up to the stoop were agony. Pushing the lobby door open was almost more than I had strength for.

I staggered inside, vaguely aware that the lobby light seemed to have burned out. Had to happen sometime.

Three forms came at me, shadows in the dim light from the street. They were wearing ski masks.

SIXTEEN

THE NEAREST ONE was large and a lot taller than I. When he grabbed me, I used technique number 37, picking my feet off the floor. Surprised that he was holding my whole weight, he fell forward. I shouldered him into the second man as he fell, and our combined weights tossed the second guy against the wall. The third was on my back by then. I did another fall, then stood suddenly, driving the top of my head into his chin. He tumbled backward.

But I hardly realized it. People who've had concussions in the last week shouldn't try to use their heads.

The world was pulsing again in pink and lavender. There was pain all down my neck and into my spinal column. Not being able to see, I did what I should have done while everything else was happening. Scream. Yell for help. Wake somebody up.

But the man's hand was over my mouth in an instant. His arm was around my upper body. And even as I realized that, another one of them picked up my feet.

They had not spoken word one.

They carried me out the door. There was a bumping as we went down the steps. Once outside, I heard one of them start to groan. Very professional of him to have held off until we were outdoors. In a spitting whisper, he said, "I think she broke my jaw!"

"Be quiet and come on."

"I'm gonna kill her."

"You're going to leave her alone and drive."

They carried me maybe half a block along the sidewalk.

Just when the pink and lavender starbursts stopped and I thought I was going to start seeing again, they dropped me to the pavement, and one of them put a knitted stocking cap over my head backward. He didn't let go of my mouth for long. Then I was carried like a sack of meal again. A car door opened. I was dropped in. A body got in next to me, and the door slammed.

The car started.

The pain in my head was just as bad as it had been, but the lights in front of my eyes were gone. My best bet probably was to play possum for a few minutes. Figure out where everybody was sitting. Gather some strength. Then pounce with the ferocity of a puma.

Don't I wish! I felt as if I'd been through a garbage disposal.

We stopped. We couldn't have gone more than five or six blocks—which, in this part of the world, can change the scenery considerably. If they were going to shoot me and dump me someplace, this was the time for me to spring.

"This is a warning," the man I thought of as the boss whispered to me firmly. "Quit. Be smart."

That sounded good. The dead don't need warnings.

But then, who knew what form the warning was going to take? Having a slashed face isn't so great, either. Again, I got ready to spring.

The door next to my feet opened. Before I could figure out how to kick the man who had opened it, he had wound two or three turns of rope around my ankles and was pulling me out. The other one—the one inside—held both my hands behind my back. He edged out of the car as the first one pulled me.

My head hit the side of the car as I fell out, but I twisted fast and caught the curb with my shoulder so I wouldn't strike my head another time. I was seeing sparks again.

And dizzy!

No, it wasn't dizziness. They were swinging me back and forth. They got a good swinging arc going. Then they let loose, and I sailed up into the air. For a whole second sheer terror showed me a dozen Technicolor pictures of what lay beneath. The Chicago drainage canal? Lake Michigan? A railroad track? An underpass of the Outer Drive twenty feet below? A fence with spikes?

I landed with a soggy, squashing noise. At first it felt soft. I was very much relieved.

Then the stench hit me.

I pulled the stocking cap off my head. As I did so, I sank lower into the glop, and a slimy, slippery thing covered my face. I couldn't breathe. I grabbed with my hands but caught nothing firm. Panicking, I thrashed wildly with my feet. This pushed my face above the level of the guck.

I saw a building, dark red fuzzy brick. At some distance there was a streetlight. I was above street level. I couldn't actually see the street from here, and the light looked doubled.

I was seeing double, which was why the brick looked fuzzy.

Around me was a huge box with metal sides. A Dumpster! I was mired up to my chin in plastic garbage bags. This would not have been so bad if the garbage was all inside them. But several had broken open when I was thrown in. Others broke when I tried to stand up. And a lot of the garbage had never been in bags in the first place. Fish bones, mayonnaise slime, and brownish lemon peels coated my right arm as I raised it to take hold of the Dumpster's side. I hung there for a moment, holding myself steady, to let my vision clear. With my left hand I felt around my ankles and unwound the rope. It had not been knotted.

There were coffee grounds in my hair and ears and something on my face that smelled like sweet-and-sour sauce gone rotten. I couldn't get any footing in the bottom of the thing. My best suede boots kept rolling bottles and jars around down there, and chunks of ghastly-feeling stuff that yielded squashily. The plastic bags slid back and forth in the slime as I moved.

I grabbed the metal sides with both hands, pulled up, and
looked over. The whole Dumpster swayed dangerously. I
froze in place.

Over the edge I saw what I guessed was North Avenue,
judging both by its architecture and the numbers of stores
labeled in Korean and Vietnamese. Several businesses,
mostly taverns and restaurants, were still lighted. There was
no one on the street.

These Dumpsters are very large, seven or eight feet deep
and maybe twelve feet long. Mine was about three-quarters
full, six feet deep in crud. Teenagers in Chicago are
constantly getting killed by climbing on Dumpsters and tipping them over. This one was unsteady. I had to get out
without tipping it on me and killing myself. I had a problem.

There was nobody around to call. Climbing out, my second alternative, was seriously risky. Though I'd try it before I'd go with alternative three, which was stay here in
disgusting garbage until morning or until the pickup came
by. I'd have tetanus by then or be pickled in soy sauce. Or
die of stench poisoning.

Me and my Dumpster—we were located around the side
of the building in a sort of alley. A restaurant sign in front
of the building was still lit. In the wall next to us was a window. The first floors here are built a few feet above the street
to give the basements some windows, I guess. Therefore, this
had to be a high window on a first floor, which put it ten feet
above the ground. Maybe it was high enough so they didn't
bother to lock it.

I let loose of the alley side of the Dumpster. My goal was
to make it across the sludge to the side of the Dumpster near
the wall. Not so easy. A bottle rolled away under my foot,
and I sank in the garbage again, over my head. Plastic
flapped wetly in my face. It was too much like my fears of
drowning. Panicky, I swam violently up. A scum of wet tea
leaves hit my face. There was slime in my eyes. Hot sauce

got in my nose. I nearly screamed, snorting as the fiery stuff burned.

Splattering garbage, I reached the far side. Please—let the window be open.

It wasn't. Why should it be, right near the smelly garbage? But there must have been one small fortune cookie in my Dumpster. I pushed at the window. It was unlocked.

It went up without a creak. I grabbed the windowsill and hauled myself in. Never mind how my shoulder hurt. This was sheer sensuous delight, getting clear of the garbage.

Inside was a dark, claustrophobic room, only big enough for several mops, a broom, a vacuum cleaner, and cleaning miscellany. The narrow door was closed. Light shone under it.

I smelled worse now that I was out of the garbage and all that refuse was hitting the air. Never mind. I opened the door.

In a big glossy white room were lots of shiny steel saucepans and shiny frying pans and woks hanging from the ceiling. It was hard to see, the light was so bright. Steam rose at the far end from a huge dishwasher. Down the middle of the room ran a long pale wood table, and all around it sat an Oriental family, from smallest baby to senior grandfather.

They had to be the owners of the restaurant, finishing off whatever had not been needed in the dining room that night. Now they were all staring at the Ugly Monster from the Broom Closet.

"Sorry," I said. "Wrong turn."

"Yes, yes," said the senior woman, rising.

"Is the exit this way?" I asked.

"Yes, yes," she said. "Exit. Yes, yes!"

"Thank you."

I hurried through the swinging door and found myself in the restaurant, where five or six patrons were finishing their dinners. The smell of me would curdle their meal if I don't move fast.

"Took a wrong turn," I said, bobbing my head. "Sorry."
And I hurried out the door.

THE SIGNPOST ON the corner confirmed it was North Avenue. Only five blocks from home. Good. No taxi would pick me up, anyway, smelling and dripping like this.

Scraping coffee grounds from my hair and sauces from my clothes, I trudged home. At one corner I stopped and shook like a wet dog. Disgusting things flew off in all directions. A misty rain started to fall. A little farther along I checked my back pocket for my wallet and my collection of pencils and pens. All there, as far as I could tell.

Slime squished in my boots. Unspeakable table scrapings ran down inside my shirt in back. But there was my door. Home. If any assailants lay in wait in the hall, I'd just hug them and pollute them to death.

My God, there *was* somebody in the hall.

An odd mugger, to wear a three-piece suit in charcoal gray with a chalk stripe.

"I called and called, and then I got worried," he said. "John!"

SEVENTEEN

JOHN MADE THE coffee for breakfast, but I scrambled the eggs and warmed the croissants. He's a bit of a conservative about gender roles. He's a bit of a conservative about everything else, too. But he's sweet. I was wearing cowboy boots and denim. My best suede boots were dead as doornails, on their way to that great resole shop in the sky.

"Now," he said, sitting there in his white shirt, creased pants, vest, and blue-and-red-striped tie, "I want you to call your neurologist."

"Are you dressed in a way you believe to be informal?"

"Certainly. I don't have my jacket on. Don't change the subject. I want you to call your neurologist."

"Why?"

"Do you remember how you felt last night? When you came in, your head hurt so badly you could hardly see."

"Well, I'd been hit."

"Exactly. Too soon after a concussion. So call your neurologist."

"What'll you do if I don't?"

"I'll hold my breath until I turn blue."

"When you lose consciousness, you'll start breathing again."

"I'll leave my tie off at work"—he grinned—"and feel miserable all day."

"I'll call."

The hospital said that Dr. Fuzzy Cheek was making rounds. They'd beep him. I held.

He came on and remembered me. Gratifying. "Am I supposed to still be having headaches?" I asked.

"Well, it's only been—what?—a week. Yeah, you sure could."

"I sure am." John could not hear what the doctor was saying, but he mouthed, *Hit on head.* "I got a sort of hit on the head," I said.

"When, where, and how hard?"

"On the side of a car. On the side of my head. I sort of fell. Not too hard."

"Having any double vision?"

I thought of the instant when I first stood up in the Dumpster. But it had gone and not come back.

"No."

"Nausea? Numbness anywhere? Difficulty coordinating?"

"No."

"Listen, why don't you just come in when you're in the neighborhood? It doesn't sound grave, but I'd feel a lot better if I had a chance just to look at the situation. The best time to catch me here is after two in the afternoon."

"After two and before when?"

"I hardly ever leave."

"Oh, okay."

I hung up.

"He says it doesn't sound grave."

"Mmm-mm? Didn't he also say he wants to see you?"

"At my convenience."

"And you'll see him?"

"Yes. But maybe not today."

"Cat, look at me. You are an adult. I am trusting you not to wait until you're hauled off on a stretcher," John said, rising. "I have to get to work."

"Do you *have* to? On Saturday?"

"The market's closed on Saturday. Which gives us quiet time to make sure the back room is operating right. Also, we take orders on Saturday. For Monday buys and sells first thing. It gives us a competitive edge."

"I wanted to get your opinion on something."

"Okay. Let me call the office and have somebody cover for me."

"No, no. It's your job."

"Human concerns are more important. Junior Genius had been wanting to cover, anyway."

"Junior Genius?"

"His name's Junior Jenrette. Twenty-one-year-old whiz kid. He's a nut." In a matter of seconds, John got Junior on the phone. "Don't take orders for anything unless the customer specifically requests it," he said. Junior must have objected, because he said even more firmly, "That goes for sales, too. Don't *suggest* anything. Don't think. I'll be there soon. *Don't get cute.*"

"I STARTED OUT WITH less than ten possibles in the bombing," I said to John. "There were fewer than twenty people in the reception room to begin with, and about ten of them were eliminated by me or McCoo. One or two were organizers of the bash. A college official or two. Not committed to any point of view, as far as I could see, anyway. When you got right down to it, there were only nine that even seemed possible."

"Okay. Who were they?"

"One: Glen Barton. He's high up in the DEA, the Drug Enforcement Administration, and he was speaking in favor of tough laws."

"Naturally."

"Two: Leota Parks. Chair of the northern Illinois PTA. She's about fifty-five, schoolteacherly. She was going to speak. Very pro very tough laws."

"Mmm-mm."

"Three: Max Sugarman. Louise's husband, of course. He wasn't a speaker; his wife was. He was for repeal, natch."

"Go on."

"Four: Professor Cameron Lloyd. Psychologist. One of the speakers. In favor of repeal.

"Five: Professor Robert Erdmann. Also a speaker. Also pro-repeal.

"Six: Charles Jaffee. He was speaking on treatment centers. He's more or less neutral, I guess. He's Joe Jaffee's son."

"I know who he is."

"Oh, sure. Seven: Torkel Gates. He's my Uncle Ben's assistant in PASA. In favor of criminal penalties. He wasn't going to speak.

"Eight: Uncle Ben Hoskinson. Head of PASA. In favor of tough drug laws, of course.

"Nine: Stan Gotchka. Head of the Chicago Police Department drug squad. He's in favor—um, against—well, at least he was going to speak about the enforcement of the drug laws."

"Fine. Let's clear the decks. Are there any of these you've definitely eliminated?"

"Charles Jaffee is eliminated because he could not have triggered the detonating device. Stan Gotchka I eliminated last night."

"How?"

"He's spent the last three or four months in an off-again, on-again wrangle with his wife. Everybody in his office knows about it. He's a wreck. It must have been eating at him for a long time. I don't think he had any emotional energy left over to blow up Louise Sugarman on the theory that she threatened his job. And she didn't really threaten his job, only his assignment. If the drug laws were repealed, he'd just be reassigned to homicide or waterfront, or something, anyway. And he'd prefer it. He doesn't want to do drug enforcement. He thinks the people he's arresting are more sad than criminal."

"Okay."

"And if that wasn't enough, when I mentioned Louise, for a second he couldn't remember who she was."

"I'm convinced. Eliminate him. That leaves seven."

"Glen Barton. Leota Parks. Max Sugarman. Cameron Lloyd. Robert Erdmann. Torkel Gates. Ben Hoskinson.''

"Let me bottom-line. Motive-wise what you're thinking is this: Glen Barton is afraid of losing his job, or the whole agency could fold. Leota Parks's motive is hatred. Max Sugarman—either envy or personal hatred, or he wanted Louise's job. You think Cameron Lloyd wanted her job. You think Robert Erdmann wanted her job. Torkel Gates may have hated her views. Ben Hoskinson hated her views."

"Yup. In a nutshell."

"I think you can reduce it one more. If the DEA, or any agency, or any agent of any agency, were crazy enough to murder the opposition, they would not have one of their own in the room."

"If it were an agency thing, I guess. But suppose Barton is just a lone nut?"

"He'd still have access to a lot more subtle ways of doing it. Cat, in my job I don't handle only private portfolios. I direct a couple of major funds, too. And very odd things happen in governmental agencies. Like they do in multinational corporations. Crooked things *do* happen. But these agents are usually very slick people—"

"This one's slicker than a banana peel on Teflon."

"Then my bet is this is not his job."

"I'll buy it. Temporarily. Leaving Leota Parks, Max Sugarman, Cameron Lloyd, Robert Erdmann, Torkel Gates, and my uncle Ben."

"I wish I could see a solid financial motive. I always find them *very* convincing."

"But as it is, what do you think?"

"Bottom-line? A guess?"

"Yeah. Go ahead."

"I've met Erdmann. He's ruthless enough for anything."

WE KILLED THE whole pot of coffee.

"I don't know how I'm ever going to break the facts loose about the bombing if it's one of those six," I said.

"Well, don't."

"What?"

"It's not your job. You're a reporter, not a policeman."

"I *want* to break the case. From inside. It'd be the story of the year!"

"If you survived. Cat, those men who picked you up last night didn't need to warn you. They could just as easily have killed you."

"Sure! You bet! So what?"

"So I want you to give it up."

"Well, you're just out of line, that's all!" I was getting angry, and he knew it.

"Cat?"

"Yes?"

"I know you think I'm pretty stuffy at times—"

"Not exactly—"

"It's true. And you think I'm conservative and rigid and old-fashioned. But think about what it is I'm in favor of. I'm in favor of you going on living. I'm in favor of you and me being married or at least being—you should pardon the expression—committed to each other."

Hell. "That's sounding kind of good these days." But I thought I'd better break off this subject. "John! Look at the time!"

"Ten-thirty."

"You're two hours late! It's all my fault."

"It's okay."

"But it's your *job*."

"Doesn't matter. You're more important."

EIGHTEEN

IT WOULD BE NICE if life were easier to decode. If people were either all good or all bad. If the arguments on an issue were all on one side. But I suppose then there wouldn't *be* an issue.

I spent an hour after John left working on the early drafts of the two articles. The one about Louise Sugarman was languishing. It had a very satisfactory opening—750 words on the explosion. Lots of immediacy—after all, I was there. Not so satisfactory was the next part, a sketchy account of what little was known of her life. I would talk with Max again about her. But I was becoming very doubtful about whether anything I got from him was really trustworthy.

And after that point, the article trailed off to nothing. I didn't know any more about who set that bomb than I had a week ago. As a Pulitzer-winning piece on how and why she was killed, it didn't make it.

The article on the legalization debate was much better. It worked because there were two points of view and real people—honest, well-meaning, and thinking people—might hold either view. I had formatted it as a debate, in this draft, in spite of what Mike thought. It seemed to work, though I didn't have a real opening. I needed a grabber. It needed more research and a lot of rewriting, too, but it would sell.

Long John Silver soared over and perched on the monitor of my word processor system. He said, "*Awwk!* What light from yonder window breaks?"

Dropping both versions on the desk, I went to the window. The day was sunny and clean after the misty rain last night. It looked like one of those beautiful Indian summer September days.

But I didn't want to go out. I felt scared and uneasy. Sort of a generalized apprehension.

This was obviously an aftermath of the events last night. You can't give in to that kind of fear if you're going to do any investigative reporting. It's a matter of getting right back on the horse.

I decided not only to go out immediately but to walk, too. That's the way to work out sore muscles.

On the street, my eyes kept watching for shadowy figures just out of view. My brain kept telling me I was being watched. Obviously, since last night, my brain could be right. I might have been watched for several days. But there was nothing to be done about it.

On with the research. Going to PASA would kill two birds with one stone. Pardon me, LJ. They'd probably have some statistics I could use for article number two. And as for who killed Louise Sugarman, both Torkel and Uncle Ben were still in the running.

But Uncle Ben wasn't at PASA headquarters. They said he hadn't come in this morning.

All right. Let's get this thing over with. It was time to confront him directly. It was just too uncomfortable going around wondering whether a relative was guilty of murder. And not much minding perhaps blowing me up in the process.

UNCLE BEN'S BUILDING, while not at the very edge of the lake and therefore not the ultra-ultra, was pleasant. There was a uniformed doorman. Every apartment had a balcony facing toward the lake, which they could not quite see because of the *very* expensive building between it and them.

The doorman knew me but still buzzed Uncle Ben's and Aunt Elise's apartment on the third floor to ask if they could see me. Good security is definitely included in the price of condos around here.

"Catherine. Come in," Uncle Ben said. There wasn't a whole lot of welcome in his voice.

"Uncle Ben, we have to talk."

"Who is that, Ben?" Aunt Elise's voice came floating in from the bedroom.

"Never mind. You rest," Uncle Ben said.

"I'm not tired."

Aunt Elise drifted into the room. Floated. Glided. She looked like a Tennessee Williams heroine, in a draped peignoir of pale blue. Aunt Elise is easily my prettiest relative. At fifty-five she still has a china-doll complexion, blue eyes, and pretty, curling blond hair.

"Hello, Aunt Elise," I said.

"Yes, hello," she said dreamily. "Who are you?"

"Um . . . I'm Catherine, Aunt Elise."

"Oh? Yes?"

Uncle Ben said, "Go back to bed, Elise. The doctor will be here soon, and I'll bring him in."

"Oh, yes. Is it almost noon?"

"Yes. You go ahead now."

She floated away like smoke. I stared fixedly at a chair. Ben was staring at a lamp. Then he walked out on the balcony through the glass doors, and I followed.

He stood looking over the city, toward the invisible lake. I looked down and saw the round cap on the doorman's head, saw him flag a cab for a resident. The silence dragged out.

"Nice geraniums," I said. They were set all along the brick railing of the balcony in a row of circular wire holders. The holders had been bolted to the wall, but the geraniums in their pots sat loosely in the circles. "Don't they blow off in wind storms?"

"No. Anyway, that's why they're in plastic pots. If they fell on somebody, they wouldn't hurt him."

"Well—" I said.

I couldn't think of much else to say about the geraniums. I'm not good at small talk. My mother would have said, "Oh, how wonderful! I just don't have any *luck* with geraniums."

Uncle Ben came back from the balcony and sat in one of the wrought-iron chairs. I sat in another. Slowly, he took out a cigar, peeled the wrapper, clipped the end, lit it, and puffed, a big puff of blue-gray smoke.

"Well, now you know why I'm sometimes not at headquarters."

"I guess. What's wrong with her?"

He closed his eyes, opened them again. He sighed. "She's addicted to tranquilizers."

"Oh."

" 'Oh' is right. Ironic, isn't it?"

"Yes, sort of. What are you doing about it?"

"There's a doctor who lives in the building who's trying to reduce the amount she takes. It's a very slow process. She becomes agitated and frantic if she doesn't get enough. His office is a block away, so he comes home for lunch, anyway, and comes up and sees her afterward. That's who we were waiting for when you arrived."

"Why not take her to some hospital that specializes in drug treatment? Like the Betty Ford Center."

"She won't go. She's scared of hospitals."

I couldn't much blame her there. "Is it working? Reducing the amount?"

"He's got the Dalmane reduced to about half, and the tranquilizer is down about a third. She doesn't sleep without the stuff, and she wanders around all night, gets all jumpy, and starts hyperventilating. She *did,* that is, until he hit on just how much he could reduce it without her feeling the difference. But sometimes I don't get to PASA because I have to have somebody here when I'm out."

"Why?"

"Because of the balcony."

I looked over and shivered. Four floors. It was enough.

In my head, I started to put all this together with Louise Sugarman. Uncle Ben was not an irrational man. In the last few days I had learned that he was more pragmatic than I would have guessed. If he was able to say Elise needed treatment for a problem with a legal drug, I just didn't believe that he would hate people who had problems with illegal drugs. I doubted that he would hate a person who would put more drugs in the legal category.

I could ask flat out. And usually that's the best way to find out anything. But I knew he was uncomfortable with my walking in on his personal problem, and I didn't want to tell him, on top of it, that I suspected him of blowing somebody up. So I just said, "What did you really think of Louise Sugarman?"

"She was wrong. But she meant well. And she was a nice person."

"What kind of nice?"

"She never fought dirty. She never called her opposition names. They called her some, I can tell you. She never distorted figures."

"What figures?"

"You know, a lot of people in the middle of a debate will make up numbers on the spur of the moment. They call the percentages the way they want them to be. You'd be surprised how often they get away with it. There are people even on *my* side of the debate who do it." He smiled, just a little, then puffed his cigar. He said, "Louise was straight."

You never really know what another human being is thinking, of course. But you still have to make decisions and run your life on the basis of your best guess, aided by whatever facts you can get. I *did not believe* Uncle Ben hated Louise Sugarman.

Therefore, since there were only twenty-four hours in the day, anyway, I was going to take up the next candidate on the list. Torkel Gates.

"Uncle Ben, I've been worried about Torkel."

"Why in heaven's name would anybody be worried about Torkel?"

"Um—" In for a penny, in for a pound. "You don't think there's any possibility he could have set that bomb?"

Uncle Ben looked at me as if I were nuts. Bonkers. Not firing on all thrusters.

"You're joking, Catherine—aren't you?"

"Well, no."

"But how could he? How would he figure it out?" He looked closer at me. "You know about Torkel, don't you?"

"What do you mean, know about him?"

"Torkel is mildly retarded."

HOOOOHH-KAY!

We sat there for another couple of minutes in what came close to companionable silence. Then Uncle Ben said, "He can read and drive a car. He got his driver's license the ninth time he took the test. He graduated from high school in five years in mostly remedial classes. He works as a maintenance man at Hair Apparent, that trendy barbershop on Michigan. He loves working for PASA in his spare time and taking brochures around."

"Oh."

"But I can't picture him doing anything complicated."

I WALKED SOUTH FROM Uncle Ben's, along the Outer Drive where Lake Michigan is cupped in the curve of the Chicago skyline. Where the Outer Drive curves away and Michigan Avenue begins its plunge into hundreds of millions of dollars of real estate, I went straight. Along the sidewalks were the trees that in two months would sparkle with tiny white Christmas lights. Right now it must have been seventy degrees in the sunshine. The Magnificent Mile. Michigan Boulevard. The Boul Mich. Absently, I looked in store windows as I walked. A black car, its reflection wavy in the glass, slowed as it went past behind me. It turned a corner up ahead.

Probably looking for some street or shop.

I studied a display of Pawley's Island rope hammocks in the Crate and Barrel window. My apartment definitely would not accommodate a rope hammock. Idly, I wondered what it would be like to live in the country. Also, what it would be like to have time to lie in a hammock.

In the window, I saw the black car stop behind me.

Two men got out. I whirled around.

They weren't in uniform, but their faces, their voices, and their walk said, "Cop."

"Catherine Marsala?" said one.

"Yes?"

"Lieutenant Gotchka wants to see you." He held out his ID. It also said Cop.

"Well, tell him I'll be in later today. Or maybe tomorrow."

"He wants to see you now," said the short one.

"Get in the car, ma'am," said the other.

Ah, he speaks!

If he hadn't said it that way, I wouldn't have been annoyed.

"Tell Gotchka I'll be in when I'm good and ready!"

They moved closer. One stood on each side of me, and they stared down. They outweighed me. They were much taller. They were also armed.

"GODDAMMIT, STAN! What's the big idea?"

"What's what big idea? Pevsner—hold it right there! What exactly did you do?"

"You said pick her up, we picked her up."

"I said see if you can find her and offer her a ride here."

"Yeah. That's what I said. You said pick her up."

"That is *not* 'pick her up.' "

"I thought you meant it—uh—like you meant it—um—like—"

"Euphemistically?" I suggested.

"Yeah!"

Gotchka said, "Next time, Pevsner, you will not interpret. You will not even try to think! You will simply *do exactly as I say!*"

STAN WAS LOOKING a little puffy. His eyes were red. His temper wasn't so hot, either. But he was also in the post-binge contrite stage.

"I'm sorry, Cat."

"You should be."

"I never intended—"

"Okay, okay. I'm not mad anymore. What are you doing at work on Saturday?"

"I might as well be," he said. He was fidgety. "I mean, I'm sorry about last night, too. You helped me out last night, you know, Cat. I needed to blow off some steam."

"Yeah, I know."

"Cat, did I say anything—?" He stopped.

"What, Stan?"

"Anything about, um, my work?"

Oho. Curious, I said, "Yes, you did."

"What sort of thing?"

This was very interesting. "What are you worried about, Stan?"

"I just didn't want anything to get back. A person in my job can't be—uh—lukewarm— Hell! We were just having fun, huh? Off the record."

"Stan, look deep into my eyes. I do *not* get stories that way. At least not from honest people. Whatever you said, it isn't going into print."

He smiled, finally, wincing as he did, but still it was a real smile. "I knew that," he said.

Sure. "Do me a favor, then?"

"You bet."

"At the University of Chicago reception. Just before the bomb went off?"

"Yeah?"

"You were maybe fifteen feet away from me, so you had a different perspective on the room. What did you see?"

"Well, let me think. I can remember a lot about the instant after the bomb blew."

"No doubt. But that's not what I want."

"See, before it, I was talking with somebody and pretty much paying attention to what he was saying."

"Who was it?"

"Her husband."

"Max Sugarman?"

"Yeah."

"Which way were you facing?"

"I was facing you."

"And you were in intense conversation with him?"

"Well, that is not a very intense man. But we were talking."

"So he was facing—?"

"Away from you."

SCRATCH MAX SUGARMAN. You can't detonate a bomb with an infrared pulse without aiming the pulse at the sensor.

WELL, WASN'T THIS what I wanted? To cut down the list of suspects? I walked toward the elevators at the Chicago Police Department, thinking furiously. If I eliminated Torkel and Uncle Ben and Max Sugarman—and Lord knew that was what I was trying to do, exclude one after the other until I got down to one—that left Dr. Cameron Lloyd, Professor Robert Erdmann, and Leota Parks.

As long as I was here in the copshop, why not stop in on McCoo?

Maybe McCoo had come up with something. The Chicago bomb squad is excellent at collecting technical evidence at crime scenes. And McCoo would be pushing his detectives for a solution. It would look bad unsolved. It was the kind of case he got his teeth into personally.

Besides, that, I could ask him about drug enforcement, too. While the article on Louise Sugarman was hanging fire

until I solved the murder, which, by God, I was going to do,
I had to get the repeal-debate piece in shape to sell. There
was rent to pay and food to buy.

NINETEEN

"McCoo, I NEED to know something."

"Sure, Cat."

"This war on drugs. Is it working?"

With most of my black friends, it's not as easy to tell when the blood rushes to their face. With McCoo, his eyes turn pink. Right now his eyes turned red.

"Come with me," he said.

We marched down the hall to the detective's room. "Bramble!" he shouted. "Over here."

Bramble proved to be a woman police officer. She got there on the double. Everybody else in the room was paralyzed at McCoo's tone.

"Take this lady," he said to Bramble in a tightly controlled voice, "into a room and search her. You are not searching for a weapon, understand?"

"Yes, sir," said Bramble, who clearly did not understand.

"You are searching her for a wire. You are to do a much more thorough search than for a weapon."

"Yes, sir," said Bramble, her eyebrows rising up to her Afro.

"I'll wait."

"Yes, *sir*."

We went into the woman's rest room. I stripped, on her orders. We were both embarrassed.

"You're not wearing a wire."

"I know that."

"Why's he doing this?"

"I don't know."

"You a reporter?"

"Yes. But I'm not that kind of reporter."

Finally, she ran her hands through my hair. No wire. She felt over my clothes, boots, my dozen pens and dozen pencils.

"Why so many pens and pencils?" she asked.

"It's a compulsion. Or a phobia. Mania. I don't really know why."

She handed them back. "It's my job on the line if you've got any really weird secret hiding place—"

"I haven't. I haven't."

I came out expecting a modest apology from McCoo. No such thing. He barked, "Follow me," and went for the stairs.

We went down. And down and down. His office is on the thirteenth floor. We went down to the basement. There was this little cement room with piles of paper in damp, bulging corrugated boxes.

"This where you guys do the third degree, McCoo?"

"No," he snarled.

"Jeez! All I did is ask you a question. No call to get angry at me."

"I'm not angry at you."

"And you know I play fair. Why would I secretly record anything you'd say?"

"You wouldn't. Ninety-nine percent probable. It's the one percent that I'm watching for."

"What's to stop me quoting you *without* a tape?"

"Oh, c'mon, Cat!"

"What? What would be the difference?"

"Deniability."

"Oh…Tell you what, McCoo. *You* do this interview. God knows we aren't getting anywhere this way."

"You remember what you asked?"

"Yeah, this war on drugs. Is it working?"

"Does it *look* like it's working?"

"Um—"

"Cat, are you working on Sugarman or what?"

"What. Well, both, actually. I've been submerged in the repeal debate, without intending to be. I mean, all I started out doing was a simple profile of Louise Sugarman. So now I think at least one thing I'll get out of all this work is an article on the pros and cons of repeal."

"Do you have any idea what you're getting into?"

"Sure."

"Oh, sure! Do you realize how much money is tied up in this business?"

"Drugs are a multi-million-dollar business—"

"No, no. In antilegalizaton."

"What do you mean? The mob?"

"Them, too. Them mostly. But also apparently legit businesses. Listen, Cat, one of Chicago's top law firms is going to start drug testing its employees."

"I heard that. They'd better do alcohol testing while they're at it."

"Pay attention. Let's just imagine, and it doesn't take much imagination, that city employees, or at least transit employees and such, are going to be drug tested."

"Okay."

"Let's say a complete profile—really complete, meaning marijuana, cocaine, heroin, LSD, PCP, two dozen other designer drugs, speed, plus legal drugs illegally obtained— let's say such a test ran around a hundred and fifty dollars a test."

"Yeah, let's say that."

"Let's say they test ten thousand city employees. How much money is that?"

"Um—just a second—$1.5 million."

"Okay. That's going to go to some laboratory here in Chicago, right? Say it's two or three labs. You think it's not in their interest to keep the public hyped up on the question?"

"Yeah, I see."

"You think they're going to love you doing a rational debate on it?"

"Possibly not."

"Shit, Cat!"

He went and sat down on a box. So did I.

"Testing is only a small part of it. But it's a small part of a gigantic business. There is *enormous* money out there that depends on keeping the war on drugs the way it is. Me, I don't want stoned railroad engineers or airline pilots, but I don't want them drunk, either, or whacked out of their skulls on cold medicine. Legal hasn't got anything to do with it. But it's the scare factor that gets the public programs funded."

"But, McCoo, what do *you* think?"

"Me? I think that nobody forces anybody to take drugs. You don't get tied down and told to snort a line. It's a victimless crime, and that makes it a bitch. It corrupts police departments to try to enforce a thing where people only hurt themselves."

"Okay."

"But that isn't what really makes me mad."

"Sir, I would very much like to know what makes you mad."

"What makes me mad is what it's doing to the black community. And particularly the young.

"You take a lot of young people brought up in the ghetto and they're sent to overcrowded schools, and they live in areas where there's no industry and hardly any jobs, and they have to commute an hour and a half each way to get to jobs that pay minimum wage and have no future, and they can take home maybe half minimum wage after taxes and transportation are subtracted, and you tell them all they have to do is sell this stuff, or even transport this stuff, which everybody is able to get, anyway, whatever they do, and they'll make enough money for cars and clothes and houses and jewels and furs like they'd never dreamed.

"You think *that* isn't corrupting people? Then they get drawn into the mobs, or they go head-to-head against the mobs and sell on their own, and they get tortured to death and hung up on a meat hook. And then people say, 'Oh, hell, serves them right. They're drug pushers.'

"And if that isn't exploitation! And the whole thing is unnecessary. And futile. The prices are high because the stuff is illegal. Crime and violence come in because it's illegal. But the actual effects on the person are no different than the effects of hundreds of legal drugs.

"You talk about breeding crime!" He jumped up.

"Then you get these kingpin drug dealers who drive around in their gold-plated Cadillacs and throw money to the crowd, and they're the role models for the young people. And you see some black drug kingpin gunned down, and the next thing you know he's being buried in a gold-plated casket designed to look like a Cadillac, and he's got hundred-dollar bills between his fingers. And it's on the evening news on every channel.

"And you know all over the city middle-class blacks are *wincing!* They're figuring all the white people are saying, 'Oh, that's how the blacks live.' We've got a larger black middle class now than ever before, and they've got to have this millstone around their necks. It's not only the poor blacks who get drawn into selling the crap who're hurt; it's everyone.

"Let alone the corruption in the department and the corruption in the Coast Guard and the corruption in the U.S. Customs Service. And the money! Good God, the *money* that's pouring out!"

I took a breath, and I hadn't even been talking. McCoo turned away and hit a box with his fist. It burst open, and thousands and thousands of three-by-five cards cascaded slowly to the floor.

"Parking-ticket records?" I asked.

"Probably fixed parking-ticket records."

"Don't have apoplexy, McCoo. If I have to call the paramedics, they'll think I hit you and lock me up."

"You ought to be locked up."

"Why?"

"Don't you hear what I'm telling you? Billions of dollars depend on keeping certain popular drugs illegal. The folks who want the status quo range everywhere from perfectly legitimate businesses to people so nasty and so powerful you don't want them to know you exist. These guys play hardball. You can get killed."

"But, McCoo, I'm not taking sides. I'm just laying out the arguments."

He smiled at me with infinite pity.

BEFORE I LEFT THE Chicago PD building, I asked McCoo for a favor. I had just thought, at last, of the way to open my article. A grabber.

"McCoo, is somebody around here interrogating a pusher?"

"I don't know. Are you still going ahead with this?"

I grabbed his fist and held it.

"Listen, please. I'm not stubborn just for the sheer hell of it—"

"Yes, you are."

"Well, whatever. Even if I were, this is different. I can't back away from a piece I'm writing just because somebody isn't going to like it. Don't you see that? You must have felt that way when you were a patrolman. Some guy wanted to scare you and you had to stand your ground. This is my work. Please, come on, tell me you understand that."

"I understand. There are still times not to be a fool."

"Find me a pusher in the building."

"There may not be any. Probably most of 'em are at the criminal courts at Twenty-sixth and California."

"I know where the criminal courts are. That's for people testifying or being tried. I want somebody who is here because some cop is getting leads from him. That kind of thing."

McCoo stood with his arms folded a few seconds. He went to his desk phone and said a few words. We waited, drinking his good coffee, and in about five minutes there was a call. He jotted down an office number. Pushed it across the desk. Then he said, "Cat, if you get into serious trouble and need to call the cops, tell them you're doing something for me. Use my name. It might get you help quicker."

TWENTY

"I AIN' NO PUSHER!" the man told me.

I said, "Well, then, let's just suppose. *Suppose* you were a pusher—"

"I ain' no *pusher.*"

"Pretend. Just pretend you're a pusher for a minute and answer one question. Would you do it if there weren't any money in it?"

"What? No *money?*"

"Pretend you're a pusher and there's no money in it. Would you do it?"

"Whad I take this kina risk for, there ain' no money in it?"

I HAD MY GRABBER. That was fine as far as the repeal-debate article was concerned, but what about avenging Louise? And avenging my own battered head.

This led me to realize that my head hadn't ached all day. Maybe I could get by without going to the neurologist at all. Of course, I'd promised John. Or hadn't I promised? Had I, maybe, just said I would if I could?

Well, I'd play fair with him. I'd ask him. And if I had promised, I would have to follow through.

The Chicago Police Department is on south State Street, below the high-rent district. The sidewalks are cracked and tilted. Most of the storefronts are bars, cheap diners, or billiard halls.

But the area is also gentrifying. There are the old buildings, neglected for decades but built of good brick and carved stone in the days when a lot of labor went into building. There are vacant lots. And there are the new, sleek condos made of plate glass and glossy, preformed synthetic walls. The street was like a patchwork quilt with tatty brocades and new space-age fabrics sewed together.

It was entertaining to walk through. I headed north, toward the towers of the financial district.

A brown Chevy cruised slowly past me and up on the street. It seemed to speed up when it got a block or so beyond me. But why shouldn't it? I wasn't going to imagine assassins in every passing vehicle.

It was past two, and I hadn't eaten lunch. I stopped at a stand for a Vienna red hot. Yes, I know they're not good for me.

I wandered on northward. The German mustard was great.

What more did I know now?

Dr. Lloyd, Professor Erdmann, or Leota Parks?

Leota Parks genuinely despised Louise Sugarman. Her hatred was incredible, and for that matter, I sympathized with it.

Would she have been able to get a sophisticated bomb? Sure. A mere question to any student who was a gang member or had an older brother who was a gang member would do it. If she was anything like my teacher, Miss Lamb, she could find things out without even seeming to ask, maybe while seeming to criticize gang involvement. They're very sneaky, these long-service educators. After that, she could follow up anonymously, locate a supplier, and buy the bomb. Wear a simple disguise when she went to pick it up, if she wanted to. Four sweaters for extra fat, glasses, and a wig would make her unrecognizable to most people who knew her. People who did not know her would never be able to identify her later.

And then, if she could wait a year, say, the kid she originally got the info from would have moved on to another teacher and probably have forgotten all about it.

She was short of money. But part of the reason she was short might be that she had paid for explosives.

So much for Leota Parks.

It would have been easier for Erdmann and Lloyd. As a doctor, Lloyd would have had to take some heavy chemistry courses in college. So he might have been able just to buy innocuous parts and produce an infernal device himself. For both of them, a little stiff library research would have told them the names of half a dozen revolutionary groups they could get material from, for a price. I'd done a story on these groups, too, once, in my younger days. You could even choose which end of the political spectrum you wanted to patronize, the far-right survivalists who were stockpiling weapons in the woods or the far-left radicals who hoarded detonators and gelignite and thermite lest the sudden need should arise to blow up a bank.

As the Wicked Witch of the West said, "What a world! What a world!"

THESE SPECULATIONS TOOK me through the hot dog and as far as Monroe Street. I stopped at a wire trash receptacle, wiped the mustard off my left palm, and disposed of the napkin properly. Good Citizen Cat, cleaning up the city.

It was now just a bit after three.

A brown Chevy crossed State Street from west to east at the intersection in front of me. It wasn't going especially slowly. But it looked a lot like the car I saw before.

It still might not be trouble. Anyway, I was in the middle of town. Bustle and hurly-burly and all that kind of urban stuff around me. No need to worry.

Chicago has a raft of large outdoor sculptures by heavy hitters in the art world like Picasso, Calder, and Chagall. One of them closely resembles a five-story baseball bat made out of I beams. I sat near it and considered Lloyd and Erdmann.

Erdmann could kill, I thought, for career advancement. A very competitive type. John thought so, too, and John was no fool. Erdmann had tickets for double-parking, which suggested a degree of indifference to other people's convenience. It didn't prove murder.

Dr. Cameron Lloyd was a different case. He was sincere and not apparently self-seeking. Trouble was, he was *so* sincere. You never know with idealists. Zealots. They are always wild cards. It wasn't just that he believed what he said. He believed it was important. Put more strongly, he believed young people would die if his ideas weren't implemented.

Would he kill for a chance to take his message to the people?

And how to prove it for either of them, or for Leota Parks?

One route was to find out whether any of them had withdrawn large sums of money as cash for no demonstrable purpose. This to buy the device, of course. McCoo would certainly be on to this, and he had the resources. I did know a banker, though—

Mental note: Ask the banker, Graham Fiske, to see what he could find out.

Another possibility. When this one hit me, I looked up at the sculpture. My inspiration was brilliant, as good as any artistic brainwave. Get a Carlton 120's package and a penlight. One at a time, visit the suspects. Engage them in conversation. Casually put the cigarette package down near the suspect. Casually take the penlight out of one's pocket and focus the penlight at the package. See who jumps or faints.

Ha! Genius!

I liked it a lot. It had elements of Perry Mason and Hercule Poirot and Ellery Queen. I couldn't tell John that I was going to do it. He didn't like risk.

AND THAT, BY circuitous thought, brought up John again.

Somewhere in the back of my brain there is a hook where I hang troublesome questions while they age. Then they jump out and announce answers. What had just jumped out told me that even though Mike was getting back from the Mississippi River tonight and would surely be calling, I wanted to go out with John.

YOU GO UP ON the most silent elevator the world has ever known. It's exactly like closing a door in front of you, waiting five seconds, opening it again, and the room outside has changed.

You step off the elevator, and chiseled in stone in front of you—that's right, chiseled in real Italian marble!—are the words Biller, Trueblood and Banks.

You walk past the bullpens of desks where dozens of young men and women at desks make phone calls all day long. Go under a huge stock-market ticker projected on the front wall. Take the door in the middle, and there you find John.

"Hey!" I said. "Want to do dinner?"

He smiled like an angel. Not like a stockbroker. He smiled, rose from his chair, and nodded happily several times.

I BOUGHT SOME FLOWERS on the way home, just for the fun of it. They were big, spotted orange tiger lilies. I thought it would be fun to see John's face when he realized I had spruced the place up for his visit.

The sun was getting a bit low when I turned my corner. It was only four-thirty, but the high-rises west of me start cutting off the light early.

The shadows made me look closely at my block before I got too close. No brown Chevy. No loiterers. Several perfectly safe passersby and ordinary automobile traffic.

I did the same careful check for the lobby—from outside—before entering. Thoroughly, too—peering in through the glass panel from the far left of the door and then from the far right side. Nobody was in the lobby.

I entered. As I walked upstairs, I heard Mr. Ederle's radio playing the race results. Therefore, he was home. In a crisis I could yell for him.

My phone was ringing. I opened my front door quickly, dropped the flowers on the table, ran for it—

And a black plastic bag came down over my head.

TWENTY-ONE

I KICKED BACKWARD, then batted out at the bag with both hands, stretching one side of it. But it didn't tear. The stuff is tough. Then a sharp blow hit my ankles, and I fell. A weight fell on top of me and pinned my arms.

"Stop! Stop a second!" a voice hissed in my ear. Something about the pronunciation was familiar, but I couldn't recognize the voice, because it was whispering. I wasn't even certain that it was male, though I would have bet my last Tic Tac that it was. His strength, pinioning my arms, also made me think he was male.

"There are small holes in the bag," the voice whispered. "You won't smother. Hold still a second."

I held still, but I was thinking furiously. He had been standing behind the kitchen door, of course. Waiting to jump me when I went through. Was the ringing of the phone, grabbing my attention at that moment, just a lucky accident for him? As I thought of it, I realized it was still ringing. Then it stopped.

"Yes?" whispered another voice.

The body on top of me hadn't spoken. That meant two of them. Oh, hell!

"Yes, we've got her," said assailant number two. Pause. "Half an hour."

Well, that answered that. It *was* planned.

Assailant number one, the one who was holding my arms, spoke. In a whisper.

"I can knock you out and carry you out of here like that, or you can keep still. You choose."

"All right. All right."

The whispering went on.

"We're taking you somewhere. We don't want to be seen doing it. We don't want you to see where you're going. We'd like to move you out quietly, like a sack of garbage. If you scream, we'll have to knock you out."

"Yeah, I get it."

The two mumbled together. I could imagine what their problem was. They could tie my feet and hands together and tape my mouth, but if they were seen, if anything went wrong with the operation and they were stopped getting me out, the fact that I was tied would put them in deep shit. If I was unconscious, it wouldn't look so good, either.

If they were going out on the street, they couldn't wear ski masks. It was still daylight, and they'd be plenty obvious.

What would be ideal for them was to carry a big black bag of what looked like lumpy trash, which didn't move or scream, out to their car and then vanish into the city.

What was ideal for me was to pretend to agree until they got the bag in the lobby or out on the street. And then scream bloody murder.

If these were the same guys who threw me in the Dumpster, they hadn't killed me last time. And my head certainly was not up for another bash. I'd bide my time.

"Listen," said the hissing voice. "I'll tell you again. You can make this easy. We don't want you to see us. We don't want to be seen with you. We want to take you to see a man. This doesn't have to be painful for anybody."

"Then why didn't he just invite me nicely?"

"I don't know. That's not my department. Are we gonna do this quietly?"

It was encouraging that they didn't want me to be able to identify them. After all, I wasn't hurt yet.

"Okay."

I lay still. The big lug got off me.

I was covered with a huge black plastic trash bag, with the opening around my feet. One of them shoved a couple fistfuls of crumpled newspaper in the bottom of the bag. I saw them as he pushed them in. The intent, no doubt, was to

make the whole package look lumpier and less like a hu
man body.

Now that I had been in the dark some time, I could als
see pinpoints of light coming through the bag. Sure enough
there were tiny holes. This also made me feel better. I trie
to wriggle my head toward one of the holes so that I coul
see out. It wasn't possible. The plastic was tough but limp
and every time I got my ear near a hole, the slippery plasti
slid away.

"What're you trying to do?" a voice hissed.

I didn't answer. The question wasn't repeated.

"Here we go," number one said a minute later. "Nov
listen to me and be smart. One peep out of you and w
knock you out. You may think this is a game, but you'd b
wrong."

"I *don't* think this is a game. I'm the one in the bag, yo
know what I mean?"

"Good."

One or the other of them slung me over his shoulder.
heard my front door open. If these guys had any smarts, an
somehow I thought they had a lot, the other one woul
carry a sack of garbage or piece of trash, too, just to len
color. With any luck, I might get out of this whole stupi
mess with my garbage emptied.

Just trying to keep my spirits up.

The door closed behind us. Now was the time to hold very
still and try to gauge just when the lobby door to the stree
was open. Then I would yell and burst out of the bag in th
same instant. Mr. Ederle would hear me, and people on th
street would see me. My two toughs wouldn't dare do any
thing but run.

We started down the stairs. Not yet. Wait. Wait. And lis
ten. Patience isn't easy at a time like that, but everythin
depended on hitting the right moment.

We turned left. Left? Oh, God, the back door to the al
ley! How could I have forgotten? In less than a second
whole picture flashed through my mind. I could imagine the

men cruising down the street in their brown car. Two go up to my apartment. A third takes the brown car and leaves it a block away down the alley. Then he goes to a phone booth across the street next to the Rexall. Sees me coming, sees me go in the door, waits ten seconds, then phones. Warns the men I'm coming and distracts me all in the one phone call. When the men answer the phone and tell him they've got me, he goes around back to the alley, starts the brown car, comes down the block, and waits next to the garbage cans. What more natural place for them to go with the trash?

I kicked at the bag, shrieking, lashing out with both feet, hoping Ederle heard, hoping somebody else was home, too, hoping half a dozen neighbors were milling around in the lobby with dinner guests. But in my building it wasn't likely.

I was hit. I didn't feel the blow, and the lights didn't go out; they went on. It was my old dazzling pink and lavender before my eyes. After that, I must have gone down for the count.

I WOKE UP WHEN I was dropped on a floor. Fortunately, I didn't hit my head this time but my shoulder, which was less fragile. But a pain shot through my head, anyway, and for a few minutes I was stunned.

"She shouldn't be out this long," somebody hissed.

"You ain't her doctor."

"I don't want her found in this condition." It was Number One.

"Nobody's gonna find her here."

"Caution first, brag later."

"Lemme throw some water on her."

"Don't," I said, but it came out *"Daaah."*

"See. She ain't hurt."

I groaned and rolled over. Suddenly I realized that there was no bag over my body. I opened my eyes, which apparently I'd held tightly closed against some horror.

Three men in ski masks, black turtlenecks, and black pants stood looking down at me. I raised my four hands.

They were tied together in front of me. Holy shit, double vision.

"I can't see very well," I said.

"Sammy tol' ya not to scream."

"So it's all my fault." I tried to get up on one elbow and quickly decided against it. "I can't talk to anybody now."

"Just stay there," said Number One.

"And don't try anything. Nobody's gonna hear you, anyhow."

They left and shut the door.

IT TOOK A GOOD FIVE minutes before I could really see. Meanwhile, I was trying unsuccessfully to hear what the men outside the door were saying. They were speaking in whispers even out there. Somehow that was the most frightening thing that had happened so far.

I was still dizzy, and the world seemed to lean this way and that. When I could see without my brain doubling the message, it turned out I was in a smallish room, not over five by eight feet. There were a couple of aluminum folding chairs, folded, against one wall and a case of motor oil. There was a pipe running up out of the floor and into the ceiling. Not much of a weapon here.

There was no window. Light came from a small recessed fixture in the ceiling. From where I sat on the floor, I could see the light switch next to the door.

They had tied my hands but not my feet. I shoved myself up a little farther, to sit with my back against the wall. It made me even more dizzy. I kicked at the floor, which was wood, and got an odd sort of dead sound.

And then my body turned cold.

I was not dizzy. The world was not leaning this way and that. It was too regular a sway. We leaned to what was my left, then my right, very slowly.

I was on a boat.

On water.

I hate boats, and I am terrified of being out on deep water. Since I am five feet two, anything over four and a half feet deep is what I consider deep water.

I sat pressing my back up against the wall, as if I could make it more solid, more like a *building*. Maybe I could disappear. Maybe I could fly away. Become a balloon. I jumped to my feet, staggered, and sat down again. Jumped to my feet again and tried the doorknob with both hands. Locked. No good.

Feeling sicker, I sat down on the floor. Then, just outside the door, I heard somebody whisper, "Where do you want the cement?"

YOU CANNOT FAINT when you want to. I crawled on hands and knees to the door and pressed my ear against it. Farther away, I heard another person, who sounded like Number Two, say, "Why dincha bring a bucket?"

"It's right there, you idiot," another voice whispered.

If I had not pressed my ear to the door, I would not have heard them at all. Now I wished I hadn't.

What do you need cement for on a boat?

What do you need cement and a bucket for on a boat?

TWENTY-TWO

THE ENGINES STARTED up. I could feel the thrum through the floor. Whatever I was going to do, I had to do it fast.

Then the engine died. I hoped it had sprung some very serious part, some kind of sprocket that you had to send to Mystic, Connecticut, to get. But I couldn't count on it.

I thought fast, picturing my feet in a bucket of cement. I was foolishly but thoroughly angry. Hadn't they said they wouldn't hurt me if I came with them? All right, I hadn't totally believed them. All right, I had tried to escape from them. But they hadn't meant it in the first place. They had fooled me! All that hiding their faces wasn't really as reassuring as I had hoped, either. They were just being cautious until they could be sure I would tell no tales.

Quickly, I tried to use whatever was at hand. I grabbed one of the aluminum chairs and tried to pull parts off to use as weapons. But for all that the chairs looked flimsy, they didn't come apart very easily. The bolts that held the arms to the sides bent. But when I tried pulling the arm back and forth to weaken the bolt until it broke, it just rotated in its holes and refused to yield. With my two hands so close together, I couldn't get good leverage.

I was desperate, and I decided on a desperate gamble. The pens and pencils were in my pockets where I could reach them. I pulled one out and rammed it down my right boot, vertically, next to the ankle. Then another and another, until I had surrounded the ankle with pens and pencils. I did the same with the left boot. This distended the leather a little bit, but what was more important was that it would prevent the boot tops from being pressed in against my ankles by the weight of the cement. If I could get out of the boots normally, maybe I could get out of them when they were encased in cement.

It was a gamble because I would have to acquiesce to being thrown overboard if it came to a choice between that and having the pencils discovered.

Also, it would only work if they didn't take my boots off first and if the cement didn't go over the top of the boots. How big was their bucket? And it would only work if I could keep them from discovering it.

Last, I ripped open the cases of motor oil. The cans were reasonably heavy. At least I could use them as clubs. If I had to go, I'd take some of those monsters with me.

When I decided that I had done everything I could, I waited. I was trembling. It wasn't the head injury. It was terror.

HALF AN HOUR LATER, I heard them coming. My watch said only half an hour had passed. Without a watch, I would have guessed five hours.

I heard bumping along the corridor outside. The door opened. Yellow-orange late-afternoon light reflected off the wall outside and into my room. The bumping had been a bucket three-quarters full of wet cement. Number Two clomped it down on the floor.

I hit him with the can of oil, and he went down like a sack of dirty laundry. I jumped on his back and hit out at Number One.

But he dove at me and knocked me down, and Number Three rammed my shoulder and then hit my arm, knocking the can I still held in my left hand against the wall, smashing the fingers I held it in.

Number One pulled out a gun.

The man on the floor groaned but didn't move.

"I'm done, anyway," I said, holding my head and falling to my knees. There was pain in my head and the back of my neck.

Somebody dragged me up. When I opened my eyes, I could see it was Number Three, the man who hit me. Number One unfolded an aluminum chair. I had bent it. He threw it away and got another. This one was okay, and he placed it near the pipe in the corner of the room.

"Bring her here and sit her down and hold her," he whispered.

"People will be looking for me," I said. "I have appointments this afternoon."

"They won't look here."

"And your engine isn't working."

"Sure it is."

"It went off."

"We tested it and cut it off."

Between the attack with the can of oil and constant talk, I had at least distracted him from studying my boots. He pulled over the bucket of cement and plunged both my feet in it, boots and all, up to the ankle. But not over the boot tops.

"You can't do this," I said, more loudly. This whispering was driving me nuts. Like talk around a deathbed.

"Why not?" he whispered.

"It's a cliché."

He neither laughed nor paused. He wound a length of rope around the pipe and around my knees so that I couldn't move my legs in relation to the cement. I would have wriggled, trying to disrupt it as it set, and keep my feet semifree. Then he untied my hands and retied them to the pipe.

"Hey, lookit him," said the other one.

The man I'd hit, the one I thought of as Number Two, was not moving and hadn't waked up yet. I hoped I'd killed him.

"Is he breathing?" my attendant whispered without any appearance of real concern.

"Yeah, but funny."

"Carry him aft. I'll check him in a minute."

"Aft is front, right?"

"Wrong."

"Oh."

The body got carried out the door. It left me and this character alone. I felt I knew him, but all I could be really sure of was that he didn't carry his head the way Uncle Ben did. And he sure wasn't plump little Leota Parks.

He stared at me for a minute. I hoped he was regretting it.

"You don't have to do this," I said.

"Why not?"

"I can't swim."

"Everybody can swim," he said coldly, and he went out of the room and slammed the door.

HOURS PASSED. I could feel the boat rock gently in the water. There had been a light lake breeze all day, making small waves. They had put my feet in the cement at five P.M. I could look at my watch, though I didn't really want to. They hadn't taken it, like proper muggers. It was only my death they wanted.

All the time, the cement was setting. I had tried to point my toes inside my boots, hoping to weaken the bond in the concrete around my feet. But if I was too obvious, if they saw anything wrong with it, they'd discover the pens and pencils and just redo the cement or shoot me, which wouldn't help. And short of that, my motions wouldn't make much difference. Some moisture soaked from the cement through the leather of the boots, and it was burning the skin of my feet. But that was the least of my worries.

With my hands tied to the pipe, I couldn't lean back or change my position much. And I was canted sideways at an uncomfortable angle. The longer I sat, the more my back hurt.

But that didn't really matter much, either.

What really hurt was that I couldn't keep my mind away from that deep, cold, dark water out there. The sun would have set by now. Soon we could motor out into Lake Michigan. There would be the lights of Chicago in the distance, too far away to help—

At moments I wanted to turn off my mind, now, permanently.

But then I would think, No, that's not only cowardly; it's stupid. If this is the last hour of your life, find something to enjoy about it.

That was a hard one. There wasn't much of anything edifying in this room. I thought of Mike, and I thought of John. I thought of the fun we'd had.

John would be at the apartment now, knocking on the door. He would get no answer, and he'd wonder what damn fool thing I'd done now. Would he get inside? Would he see any evidence of a struggle? Yes. He'd see the flowers, the tiger lilies, lying out of water. Would he call the police? Maybe. Probably.

Would it help? No.

If I died, I hoped he would take Long John Silver. It looked like LJ would outlive me after all. Mike wouldn't want him or wouldn't be responsible enough to take care of him.

AT EIGHT O'CLOCK on the dot, the door opened, and Number One, the boss, came in. He didn't look at me or away from me. He just stuck his thumbnail into the cement, which did not yield. He went out, this time leaving the door open. There was no reflected sunlight, and the hall outside was dark.

Was my room the only one with a light?

And why did they wait here, at the mooring, rather than start out into Lake Michigan and dump me far out of sight of land?

I thought I knew.

I couldn't be sure which of Chicago's several harbors we were in, having been unconscious when we arrived. Maybe Belmont or Jackson. But I pictured the harbors gradually emptying over the last couple of weeks. After Labor Day the boats slowly leave. The college kids who crew on the big yachts over the summer go back to school. The weather becomes colder at night. Fall storms make it dangerous for small boats. The big boats of the very rich begin like birds to go south for the winter, where their owners would meet them during the season in Palm Beach or Mexico.

So I pictured us as one lone boat, far from any neighbors, in a harbor denuded of craft. If there was no moon tonight or if it was overcast, they could slip out after dark with no running lights, dump me, and be back in half an hour. If no boat had been berthed nearby or if the owners of the boats nearby were not aboard, no one would know this boat had ever moved at all.

Not much danger of the body washing ashore, either. Most of what went down into the sands under Lake Michigan just kept on going down and was never heard of again.

The motor started.

TWENTY-THREE

THE CLUMSY ONE, Number Three, came for me. He untied my knees first, which gave me no advantage or even relief, since my feet were still frozen into the cement. When he untied my hands from the pipe, my fingers unconsciously made claws, they wanted so badly to go for his eyes or break his neck. But I would never get away from them like that, just scratching at them. Unless I saw a major chance to escape, my only hope was to keep their attention away from my feet.

I was going to give them no reason to tie my hands. Even if worse came to worst, I would rather go down with my hands free. I stretched my back, getting rid of the pain.

He dragged me to the door, with the bucket and cement thumping on the floor hurting my shins. Then, deciding that was too cumbersome, he put me over his shoulder and carried me up the ladder.

I had guessed right. We were riding on a black moonless lake with no lights. Up here, looking back down, I could scarcely see any glow from the room I had been kept in. We were invisible to the world.

The lights of Chicago were amazingly close. And heartbreakingly far. I could name them all. The great, tapering John Hancock, the Sears Building, the line of expensive condos along the Gold Coast. There were two double lines of lights on the Outer Drive where it curved away from us—red taillights and white headlights, moving gracefully. People, just arm's lengths away, it seemed, dining and strolling and driving and utterly unreachable.

I had done an article once on the harbors. Most of them had fifteen feet of water at the anchorage. Two hundred feet from shore, it fell quickly to twenty-five feet deep. We were less than a quarter mile out. What would it be? Thirty feet deep? Thirty-five feet? What difference did it make?

'Tis not so deep as a well, but 'twill serve.

Number One came from a cabin in front, where he had probably been steering the damn boat. The engine idled very quietly. Desperate, I tried once more.

"Listen! You don't have to do this! I don't know you. I can't identify you! This is unnecessary!"

They were dark figures in dark ski masks with black shirts and black pants on a moonless night. Only in the slight glow from the city did I see the one nod at the other. They did not even bother to speak. Cautious to the last. The one dragged me to the edge.

"No!" I yelled. That was a mistake. He dragged me faster.

I spoke more quietly, but gasping, "Please! Please!"

He threw me over.

THE WATER WAS COLD. I had taken a breath, fighting panic, as I went over the edge. If there was any hope at all, I had to escape in the next thirty seconds.

As I sank, eyes and mouth pressed closed, I scrabbled for my boots. The concrete came up above my ankles, but not to the tops of the cowboy boots. I had no idea if it would work or whether I could get the pens and pencils out in time.

I grabbed at the pens in the right boot, frantically, by touch alone, blind in the black night water. Desperately, I pulled one out, got hold of another, pulled it out. The leather was wet and resisted me. I couldn't get my fingers far enough down into the boot.

My body touched lake bottom softly. I was half on my side, sand washing over my hands and over the bucket. I scrabbled for pencils as fast as I could go. Eight or ten? I couldn't feel any more. Maybe that was all in the right boot. Pushing with the left foot at the cement, I pulled with the right and sucked it out. It jerked free.

I reached for the left boot. My head ached. My lungs were burning. I relieved them by letting out a little air, but I didn't have much time left. As I pulled at the pens and pencils, I realized my left hand wasn't helping. Numb and swollen from being slammed against the wall, it was no good to me.

I was dizzy. I was not sure which way was up. Would I get one foot out, only to drown, held by the other foot? I reached all around with my good right hand, tearing at anything I could get hold of.

Then, willing to tear the whole foot off if I had to, I bent my left knee, wedged my right foot against the cement block, and pushed with all my might.

Free!

I shot to the surface.

Oh, Lord, the air! I couldn't swim, never could, but for a moment I trod water with the best of them.

I looked around for the boat, trying to keep my gasping, sucking lungs quiet, but it was invisible. Less than a minute had passed. They would have motored away immediately, of course, and were now lost in the dark.

I found I could tread water. But I had to get to shore. I rolled over on my back and tried to scull. There was a light northeast breeze, which might eventually push me toward shore but unfortunately would drown me first by slapping small waves in my face. One caught me as I lay out on my back and filled my face with water and my sweatshirt with an air bubble.

An air bubble! I kicked my legs to bring me up a little and held up the shirt, catching and trapping a bigger bubble of air. Because the shirt was wet, it held the air.

My left hand was good, at least, for holding my shirt down at the waist. The bubble supported me. My right hand sculled. The waves pushed me in the general direction of shore.

To a nonswimmer, shore was a long way off, but by God, I was not going to be beaten now. I started frog kicking with my legs. Lying on my back, I took an occasional bearing on the Sears Tower but generally went on the assumption that as long as I was seeing only the dark of the lake I was heading toward the lights.

Was I making progress? It didn't look like much when I glanced over my shoulder. But I was willing to keep at it until doomsday. Or morning, whichever came first.

Then I bumped something. I felt with my right hand so as not to lose my bubble. It was a chunk of polystyrene, about twelve inches long by six by six.

Saved! Nothing could stop me now!

I PULLED MY ACHING body onto the shore pretty much in midtown. There was no one on the beach, with the exception of a "courting couple" at some distance, and I didn't want to see anybody, anyway. I was scared. Who could tell whether a lot of cronies of those three had been detailed to watch for me? The organization and the caution of those men spoke "mob" to me, let alone the fact that they had an expensive boat.

An unrelated thought came to me: I no longer felt frightened of water.

I lay shaking for several minutes on the sand, thanking the weather gods that it was September and not November. The lake water was not yet icy. Two months later I would have died of hypothermia in minutes.

As it was, I was chilled. The night was growing colder. I had to get inside quickly. I didn't want to take a cab, and anyway, my wallet was gone, lost either in the water or in one of the struggles on the boat. I couldn't go to my place. I was afraid it would be watched.

Mike's? Too far. John's? With his parents there? Hell, no. Not like this.

I looked up and the answer was almost staring me in the face. Uncle Ben's was one block north, in the building right behind the Lakeshore high-rise.

When I stood up, I realized I was not just soaking wet but barefoot. What would Ben's doorman think? Well, I was still wearing my sweatshirt top. Maybe he'd think I was a nut about jogging with my feet *au naturel*. And what did it matter, anyway? Ben would have some dry clothes of Elise's and hot coffee. What else mattered?

But I did a kind of staggering, lurching, pretend jog for that block and a half. I passed several other joggers, running the Lakeshore, who didn't even glance at me. Once I had crossed the Outer Drive, the men and women in Saturday night evening dress and fur coats certainly did give me a glance. But the sweatshirt was beginning to dry, and nobody pointed and screamed.

The doorman raised his eyebrows but said, "I'll page the Hoskinsons, Ms. Marsala." And so he did.

I rode barefoot in the elevator up to Ben's.

"Go RIGHT INTO THE bathroom," Uncle Ben said. "I'll get some dry things of Elise's."

I took off the clammy, cold things and wrapped myself in a towel. The hot water in the bathroom shower felt glorious. In a couple of minutes, Uncle Ben rapped on the door. I opened it a crack, saving his modest feelings, and he stuck a fist through the opening, with a terrycloth bathrobe, a soft sweater of Elise's, and a pair of baggy old sweatpants that looked like his.

"I'm going into the kitchen to put a kettle on," he said. "When you get dressed, go lie down on the sofa."

THE SOFA WAS SOFT; I was dry. There was a hissing scream in the kitchen, and a minute later Uncle Ben brought in cocoa. Ecstasy.

"Thanks."

"Tell me what happened, Catherine."

It was not until that instant, warm and dry, that I realized how much my feet hurt. I lifted the hem of the robe and looked at them. Ben did, too, and gasped.

"What did that to you?"

"I think it was something in the cement. It's got lime in it or some strong alkaline chemical, like lye."

"Cement! On your feet!"

"Can I tell you later? I'm so tired."

"Thank goodness I called Webber."

"What?"

"Webber. Elise's doctor. He's coming right up."

I didn't like that, but Ben might be right. He demanded to know what had happened, just a hint, before Webber arrived, so I gave him a sketchy account. "You have to call the police!" he said.

"I'm going to, Uncle Ben. But I don't know which boat, don't even know which harbor, and I don't know *who*. Let me think."

Right then the doorbell rang.

Webber looked at the feet and gasped, too. A ring of skin around the upper part of the foot and ankle had peeled entirely away, probably when I had pulled out of the cement and out of my boots. Some of the rest of the foot showed lye burns but wasn't as bad.

"I want you in a hospital," Webber said.

"In a little while. I have to do some thinking first."

"This isn't an injury you can treat at home. You may need skin grafts."

"Shit!"

"You have third-degree skin loss here. There's practically a certainty of infection. It amounts to at least thirty square inches of open wound area—"

"Listen, if I promise to go to my own doctor soon, how would that be?"

He sighed. "I'm going to give you a penicillin injection. You're not allergic? Good. And a painkiller. And some pain pills you can take."

He went ahead, efficiently, with the injections. The bottle of pain pills he left on the table.

"Now, look at me," he said.

"Right."

"You *will* call your own doctor."

"I promise."

"Tonight."

"All right."

"I won't be responsible otherwise."

"I promise. I really do."

The pain injection, whatever it was, seemed to be help
ing. Webber wrapped some sterile dressings around the an
kles, and painkiller or no, that hurt a lot. Then Uncle Ben
saw Webber to the door. I couldn't move. I was dazed. I
heard Ben thank him. They said goodnight. Ben listened to
something Webber said as he moved away. Ben said, "Two
now and two in four hours."

Then he closed the door.

"Do you want water for these pills?" he asked. "Is the
cocoa too hot?"

"No. Right now it couldn't be too hot."

He gave me two. I swallowed them with a gulp of cocoa.

"Should I say hello to Aunt Elise?" I asked.

"No, she's sleeping."

I could tell from his tone that he didn't want to talk about
her.

He let me finish the cocoa, slowly.

"Feeling better?" he said at last.

"Much."

"Feeling sleepy?"

"Very."

I put the cocoa mug down on the coffee table next to the
ashtray. Next to the ashtray in which were a stubbed-out ci
gar, Ben's, and a stubbed-out cigarette.

In the shape of a crushed *J*.

"Aunt Elise doesn't smoke, does she?" I asked stupidly.
I was starting to slur my words, with drugs or exhaustion.

"No."

He was looking past me, toward the kitchen.

I turned and saw a slender figure standing in the doorway. Charles Jaffee. Wearing a black turtleneck and black pants.

AFTER AN ETERNAL few seconds, I said, "What did you do with your ski mask?"

"Threw it overboard."

I could hardly hold my head up. The doctor couldn't possibly have meant to give me this much medication, not if he expected me to talk with my own doctor tonight. "I shouldn't have taken"—I got stuck for a moment—"those two pills."

"Not quite what he prescribed," Ben said, smiling.

"Webber—"

"Webber was in the elevator and the door had closed when I said, 'Two now and two in four hours.' The bottle says two in the morning."

"Oh."

My mind flashed for an instant to the reception at the University of Chicago, where I sat with Louise Sugarman. Why had I thought Uncle Ben was going to blow smoke in somebody's face, Groucho Marx fashion? Aiming.

I had to get to a phone, scream, do something, something quick, before I lost consciousness completely.

Jaffee was ahead of me.

"Turn on the stereo," he said to Ben. "Medium loud."

Uncle Ben did. He came back to Jaffee, who stood in front of me, looking down.

"Get her to the balcony. Hold her from behind. When you see me on the street in front, talking with the doorman, throw her over."

Ben said, attempting to be clever, "Stay and help me."

"Oh, no. I'm going to be provably out of it. But you'll be all right, too. Tell them the pain must have gotten to her. She took two extra pills when she shouldn't have. She must have become confused, wandered to the balcony, and fallen over. They'll never prove otherwise."

His voice was getting distant. My will kept saying *stay awake*, and my eyes kept closing.

"You won't even be investigated," Jaffee said.

He walked to the door. "Give me about thirty seconds to get to the lobby. Make sure you see me. Then do it. If I hold the doorman in conversation out there too long, it'll look unnatural."

He left.

TWENTY-FOUR

UNCLE BEN'S HANDS WERE shaking, but his mouth was hard and determined. "You should have dropped the investigation," he said.

I couldn't answer. My mind was racing while my muscles turned to mush. I felt a wonderful lassitude and knew it was deadly. He went behind me on the sofa, put his hands under my arms, and pulled me up over the back, across the floor, and toward the balcony. I tried to jam my feet into the floor, tried to stand up. I couldn't.

He dragged me out onto the balcony and over to the edge. He pulled me up and leaned me on the brick coping, half standing. My head was drooping, but I could see over. There he paused. Ben was looking for Jaffee. So was I.

Then a spill of light came from the opening lobby door. Voices. The doorman in his uniform and Jaffee walked onto the sidewalk, Jaffee gesturing widely.

Ben lifted me up by my waist. I wriggled, grabbing at his clothes with my hands. But I was too weak to be effective. He lifted me higher.

I fumbled for one of the geraniums and threw it over. If it had been in a clay pot, I couldn't have lifted it. I saw the doorman look up.

I threw another. There was no time for me to watch now. It was dangerous to look down. My upper body was leaning into thin air. Ben tried a great heave, lifting me almost to the top of the coping, but I hung on to his hair with my sore left hand and his shirt with my right.

He twisted, weakening his grip. I think he was trying to look over the ledge without being seen. I pulled harder on his shirt and managed to turn around head down, with my upper body inside the ledge. Upside down, I grabbed another geranium in a pot and threw it over.

Ben had his arms around my hips. I was nearly asleep, but I hugged both my arms around his knees and held on. For dear life.

In less than a minute, we heard pounding on the door of Ben's apartment.

TWENTY-FIVE

"C'MON, McCoo, you can tell me."

"I don't want to hurt your feelings, babe."

"Oh, laugh a minute. More's been hurt than my feelings already." I was still hobbling around on crutches, with skin grafts where my bobby socks ought to be. "Besides, McCoo, we don't have that kind of relationship. We're honest with each other."

"That pins me down. All right. No, I don't think your Uncle Ben cared what happened to you or to anybody else in the world but himself. You hadn't seen him all that much, even though you were cousins. Didn't you start to feel he was more self-aggrandizing than you realized?"

"I certainly got to thinking he was more competent. Maybe more aggressive than I realized. But I thought he was sincere about PASA and its goals."

"We'll never know. I don't think he'll ever admit he wasn't."

"Maybe he accepted money from the mob via Jaffee because he thought it would help the cause," I said.

"Maybe he accepted it because it kept him in power."

"Maybe Ben killed Louise Sugarman because he thought he was evil."

"And maybe pigs fly, Cat. He killed Louise Sugarman because Jaffee ordered him to. He had to follow orders because Jaffee could reveal Ben had been taking money from the mob to finance PASA. Louise had to be killed because she found it out. That was the news that was too hot to give her husband."

"Okay."

"And the mob financed your uncle Ben because the couldn't afford for repeal to go through. It would dry up th drug money that's been keeping them rich."

"Ben still may have disliked the idea of killing me."

McCoo winced and poured coffee. Finally, he said, "Ca that man is cold as ice. He never turned a hair when we a rested him. He said he thought it was a gift of fate when yo wanted to go to the reception and meet Louise Sugarman.

"How so?"

"He knew about her hip operation. He knew she'd wa to sit down. With your persistence, you might be with he He sort of hoped you'd sit on the side farther from th bomb, but not for your sake. He wanted Louise to get th full force. I take it he thought you'd both be killed."

I thought for a half minute. "Why a gift of fate?"

"That you wanted to go? He thought it would give him nice sort of proof that he hadn't done the killing, if an body suspected him. They'd know he'd never want to hu his dear niece Catherine."

"Oh. In a way I suppose that was what was wrong wit Aunt Elise."

"What?"

"She'd begun to recognize what sort of man Ben wa And didn't know what to do about it. In our family yo don't divorce. In the older generation, anyhow."

"Mmm. By the way, Cat, Ben says that Jaffee knew yo had seen him with the black box and was certain of it aft you asked a few of your casual questions. Apparently h much preferred you not ever to be able to testify about i Damn it, I *told* you you'd get yourself in trouble!"

He got up and poured me coffee. Waited on me wit cream and sugar, too. I had not told McCoo that I'd ha responded to Jaffee's romantic advances. He may have su pected it.

I said, "And what exactly was Charles Jaffee's little blac box?"

"A camera. Very subtle little gadget. It had alternate strips of regular and infrared film that wound through at twenty per second. He photographed Ben setting off the bomb. Actually photographed the infrared beam."

"In order to have something on Ben."

"Airtight proof and therefore total control of him from then on."

"I almost feel sorry for Ben."

"Don't."

"Sure. First Louise Sugarman gets him dead to rights and then Jaffee gets his balls in a vise—"

"Cat!"

"Well. And I should have guessed, because who would lose mega-billions if the price of drugs fell to zip?"

"The mob," said McCoo.

"So who has the strongest interest in fighting repeal?"

"The mob."

We sipped our coffee for a minute companionably. I had just struck a perfectly lovely deal on my story. A three-part series. Never would I have anticipated all the wonderful material this story had generated—and if I had anticipated it at the beginning and was smart, I ought to have dropped it like poison ivy.

"You never found Charlie Jaffee?" I asked.

"Not to have and to hold."

"Where is he?"

"We have it on very good authority that he's in Panama."

"I see. Working on the supply side."

MIKE WAS BACK FROM his trip, of course. John had never left. When I got home from McCoo's copshop and coffee house, I punched my answering machine.

Mike's voice: "Hey, Cat! I knew all along that Jaffee character was too slippery to be real. Anyway, now that you're back in business, I've got a great idea. Let's go west to the Mississippi for two days. My friends with the old

riverboat restaurant are doing their last banquet before
closing up for the winter. Gi'me a call.'' Beeped off. Back
on, Mike's voice again. ''No, don't gi'me a call. I don't
know where I'll be. I'll call you.''

John's voice: ''Hi. Remember—I told you if you found
out who had money riding on it, you'd find the killer. Um,
Cat, I was thinking maybe you'd need some babying. Just
for now. How about a slow, luxurious weekend at the Pal-
mer House? A play one evening, maybe a blues club. Quiet
dinners. Breakfast in bed. I'm at work now. I'll be here until six, then home, I'll call back.''

The lady or the tiger?

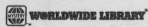

First Time in Paperback

A LOOSE CONNECTION
M.R.D. MEEK

ATTORNEY LENNOX KEMP YEARNED FOR A MURDER TO BROOD ON. WOULD HE SETTLE FOR SUICIDE?

Dorothea Copeland was a model of propriety—unlike her oldest friend, Amanda. Odd that outrageous Mandy, such a lover of life, would kill herself...especially after her delicious discovery that Queenie Mangan, someone from their past who died in a fire twenty years ago, was alive and well and dining with her husband in the Cotswolds!

A case of mistaken identity? If so, then who sent the lilies from Queenie to Mandy's funeral? If not Queenie, then who really died in that fatal blaze? Kemp suspects that Dorothea, despite her quiet ways and deliberate simplicity, is hiding dark and dangerous secrets...secrets that could be fatal to all concerned.

"M.R.D. Meek can be mentioned in the same breath as P.D. James."
—*Los Angeles Times* Book Review

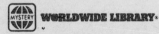